BLOOD ROSE

BLOOD ROSE

DANIELLE ROSE

OFTOMES PUBLISHING
UNITED KINGDOM

Cover art by Gwenn Danae

Cover & Interior design by Eight Little Pages

FOR MY MOM

CHAPTER
ONE

I WAS TWENTY-four years old when I was told my life was no longer truly mine—at least, that's what the prophecy said. I'd never been one for prophecies, and I rarely took the traditional Pagan path. But most importantly, I sure as hell wasn't going to let some dead elders, an ancient war, and a killer vampire race get between me and life.

My coven's high priestess, my mother, used to call me a rebel for the cause. She never spoke of any cause in particular, but since she was the most powerful spirit user we'd ever encountered (and the only witch in our coven with the ability to receive visions), I wondered if she knew of my *destiny* since the day I was born.

I was born a hereditary witch with an affinity for

spirit, and since my gift was pretty useless against vampires, I had learned to protect myself in other ways: hand to hand combat, advanced weaponry training, and good ol' common sense.

But my story didn't begin on the day I was born. My path started to form much earlier—hundreds, if not thousands, of years earlier, actually. It was that pesky ripple effect that affected every single witch and vampire to have ever lived—regardless of whether or not they actually wanted anything to do with the fight.

It all began with a war. No one *really* knew why it started or who made the first deadly move on the board. Naturally, each side blamed the other, and now, the war between mortals and immortals had all but turned to embers.

Ironically, the war led to the exposure of witches in certain villages, which then led to the witch trials that plagued the world. It's ironic because witches fought to protect humans, but when confronted with something not easily understood, the human race became outraged, murdering innocents in the hope that they'd free the world of those pesky witches.

At one point, humans believed that vampires existed,

too, which then led to nearly every culture passing down tales of demons that walked the earth hidden within the shells of humans. But vampires weren't as easy to kill as witches, and humans who witnessed the existence of *real* vampires usually died.

These days, humans didn't (or wouldn't) believe the stories of how those burned at the stake were (mostly) real witches or how there were vampires who walked in the night and fed on the living.

But as a witch, a mortal, it was my destiny to ensure that the fire remained kindled; their kind could never be (re)discovered by humans, nor could there ever be an end that allowed both species to survive. It was believed that The Power was mankind's gift from the gods, given to witches to help them fight an unfair war against immortal creatures.

With each generation, the gods blessed one witch with The Power, the ability to control all parts of nature: earth, air, fire, water, and spirit. This blessing was considered an honor and was thought to be the key to eliminating the immortal species.

However, being chosen came with a price few could bear: The Power was too much for one mortal, so the chosen witch had to be prepared to give his or her life to the cause. With each witch's death, that power and strength was passed to the next chosen one. Every previous generation had failed to eliminate the threat.

I was the chosen sixty-sixth generation witch. (Honestly, I couldn't make this stuff up. I was just one six away from Karma's cruel joke.)

My chosen status made death all too familiar. Members of my coven and community had died while attempting to protect our home, and I promised myself that I wouldn't be the next failure. I taught myself to control my ability early on. Armed with only my affinity for spirit, a gift that gave me small control over all elements, I taught myself to fight, to hunt, to kill.

My birth rite, the ritual in which I would obtain The Power, was the following eve, and to calm my nerves, my cousins and I took early to the woods that surrounded our property. I had fought vampires time and time again, but without yet being gifted, and only naturally having an affinity for spirit, I was considered too vulnerable to patrol alone. My cousins, having affinities for two of the strongest weapons against vampires, fire and air, often accompanied me while I hunted. They tagged along for bragging rights, while I fought because it was my calling.

Though I was too stubborn to admit or discuss it, I also fought because of my past. When I was a child, my father had often let me accompany him on hunts. I vaguely remembered listening to his lectures about the herbs that grew on local woodlands, the importance of dedicating myself to the craft, and the easiest ways to kill a vampire. He used to say that I'd one day save the world. He'd explained how my child self might find his teachings moot, but time would change my mind. It was Father who taught me to wield my katana, and it was Father who taught me what was necessary to kill a vampire. Aim for the head or heart, little one, he'd say. Always keep your blade close and your common sense closer. He used to say that daily, but as a child, I hadn't comprehended the true power behind that statement.

At twenty-four, I had already experienced my fair share of life. I'd had a serious relationship, a degree in biology, and a burning appetite to rid the world of vampires. Protecting those I loved was in my blood; it was the only thing I was truly good at.

The new rules in place forced me to give up the freedom I had been accustomed to. My mother would often lecture me on the dangers my hobby bestowed upon our coven. What would happen, she had asked, if the next chosen one went out and got herself killed before her birth rite? We had no idea, and my coven wouldn't risk it. My relationship with Mother drastically differed from my relationship with Father. They both held high standards, but Father spoke from the heart. Mother spoke for the coven. Even so, I often found myself wondering if her concerns of me being killed and how that would hurt the coven were just excuses. Inside, I tried to believe that she truly did fear for my life. Not because I was chosen—but because I was her only daughter.

But they knew of my strength and the benefits of patrolling, so they allowed me to continue hunting—so long as I had protection. I felt ridiculous asking my cousins to accompany me on hunts. We hadn't always had the best, or closest, relationships. But I knew they were the only ones who didn't really care to protect me. They were more concerned with themselves. Thus, it had been just like before—only now I was constantly telling someone to be quiet, to walk lighter, to breathe softer.

The forest seemed darker than usual—even at

twilight. With clouds covering the stars and moon, the gloom worked as both a benefit and hindrance while patrolling. My cousins followed closely behind me. I maneuvered around broken branches and fallen leaves with ease, while they stomped past the trees, brushing bark as they passed.

"We'll find ourselves in a mess of trouble if you two don't be quiet," I whispered.

I inhaled deeply, letting the cool air blow away my fears over my upcoming birth rite. The smell of pine was overpowering in these woods. I stretched out my arm as we walked and let the needles prick my fingertips. It wasn't enough to break skin, but it was enough to bring back feelings I had buried.

Winter solstice was drawing nearer, and soon, Mother would send me to collect pine needles for spells and decorations. She would once again explain how essential each ingredient was to our esbats. I would roll my eyes and pretend she was a bore, but inside, I cherished those moments. I wondered how many more I'd have left.

Our property stretched over ten acres of hills, forest, lake, and mountains. Mother often joked that our coven encompassed all of northern California—especially since we were trying to purchase another twenty acres. While most of our property wasn't maintained, the small part we did keep up was designated living quarters and ritual space.

Our coven only had thirteen practicing witches, but it was composed of at least three dozen people in total: the husbands and wives of practicing witches, the children too young to understand magic, and the elders too old to participate were still considered cherished members of our coven.

Our self-sufficient lifestyle had created enemies among the townsfolk—mainly because this part of northern California was rural, so local businesses relied on the resident population to keep themselves afloat. Keeping to ourselves marked us as outcasts more than we'd expected when we decided to relocate to Shasta.

I had almost forgotten that my twin cousins were trailing behind me when I heard a giggle. We were able to walk a quarter of an hour before they began making noise again. I looked straight ahead and ignored their bickering.

I felt their presence before I saw them. The wind

shifted, sending a shiver down my spine that nestled deeply in the pit of my gut. When a vampire was near, goose bumps formed, hair standing on end, and nausea was inevitable. I felt all three symptoms as I walked through the forest, my cousins slowly trailing behind me.

"They're close," I whispered.

I needed to announce their presence, even though that risked exposure. All witches could sense a vampire, but my coven was inexperienced in the craft of war. I hunted each day, willingly drawing nearer to vampires, allowing my instinctual abilities to strengthen. It only took a few months of regular patrolling to learn control of the physical side effects vampires brought with them.

I exhaled slowly, steadying my heartbeat. I knew what they were, and I knew they were out there. Somewhere.

As we reached the end of the woods, I saw them. They stood in a small clearing. I stopped so abruptly that my cousins walked into me. I raised my hand quickly, signaling for them to step backward, and they obeyed.

I grasped the handle of my katana and slowly pulled it from its sheath. The metal scraped against the leather, a noise deafening in the silence of the night. I watched them as I moved to my right and stepped behind the base of a thick pine tree.

My hair, wrapped in a tight bun, snagged on pine needles, and I bit my lip as I pulled away from the tree. Brown strands fell before my eyes. I prayed they would not hear me—even the slightest of movements would have been enough to catch their attention. I crouched beside the tree, the base wide enough to cover my body and my drawn katana.

The nearly-covered moon cast shadows over the small clearing in which the vampires stood. I silently prayed to the gods that they bless my cousins with the strength to survive this fight. Darkness was more a friend to creatures of the night. I carefully maneuvered my blade so that it would not betray my presence.

I nodded to my cousin Nina, and she called upon air. Fog thickened.

They stood in the distance—too far to touch, but too close for comfort. We were only a short walk from our sleeping quarters. They created a threat that needed to be eliminated.

There were four. Three men and a woman. The men towered over the woman, and her tiny frame was lanky in comparison to their muscular builds. Their black ensembles were strapped with blades of various lengths. Their attire was alarming. The typical vampire usually wasn't armed and often blended into society.

These four stood out. They were different.

We needed to draw nearer. We needed to eliminate the threat. I waved for my other cousin Everly to move to my side. I signaled her to encircle them in flames, and just as she lit the spark with the snap of her fingertips, I emerged from behind the tree and closed the space between us and them.

I stood behind the protection of the fire, twirling my katana in my hand.

The fire separating us only stretched a couple feet. I kept my eyes focused on them, watching for the slightest movement. We were close enough to lose our lives. But I was confident. I had yet to lose a fight, but I knew in time my confidence would get the best of me.

My internal alarms were firing at lightning-fast speeds. I had spent night after night hunting vampires, but as they stood before us now, I could see my cousins faltering. We needed to make a move—before the vampires made theirs.

"What have we here?" I said as my cousins took their places by my side. I hoped my tone wouldn't betray my forced confidence.

One vampire stepped forward, putting himself between the others and me. Normally, it would have been more difficult to determine the leader, the one who posed the biggest threat, but he made it quite simple. He was taller than the others. His tousled brown hair sat messily atop his head, a just-out-of-bed style I was sure he worked hard for. He stared as if he could read straight into one's soul. He had stubble on his jaw, as if he hadn't shaved in days. I found myself wondering how long they had been hunting in our woods.

He raised his arm as the woman behind him pulled her knife from its sheath—almost as though he predicted her temper. I met her gaze and held it, challenging her to raise her weapon. Mine had already been in hand, a move I'd learned early on. Spirit users needed a weapon to fight vampires, while theirs was always nearby and easier to pull out: fangs.

The wind picked up, blowing her blonde pixie locks from her eyes. They were blue, cold. She stared with the intensity of a killer. I promised myself I'd end her. She stood beside her leader, a good half-foot shorter than me. Her thin form showed no muscular build. I was sure I could take her easily. She gave me a knowing smile and licked her lips. Her fangs lowered, and I swallowed down the nausea.

"We don't want any trouble," the leader said as he lowered his arm. His English accent was strong and caught me off-guard. British? He was a long way from home.

"You don't belong here," I said, moving my gaze to the other two men. One bore an all-too-similar resemblance to the vampire who had just spoken, minus the perfectly messy hair. Their skin was tanned, their jaws clenched. But this vampire had his hair buzzed. I couldn't help but compare him to soldiers in our human armies. They too held an uncomfortable, challenging stare. They too were strapped with weapons. They too were ready to fight.

The final man had short, bushy black hair, dark skin, and gray eyes. He was thinner, weaker. He stood behind the others. A newborn vampire, I determined. Probably the easiest kill. I considered leaving him for Nina since she needed the practice.

"We're just passing through," the vampire said.

Inside, I was trembling—not from fear but from hatred. I couldn't believe the vampire asked for my trust, for my leniency. His kind didn't deserve such respect. They were all killers, all liars. They lived for the kill, but luckily, so did I.

"A mistake short-lived," I said. I twirled my katana and slashed it forward. I clipped the strap of a sheath, and his weapon fell to the ground. The air whipped around me as Nina called upon her element. It lashed out at the vampires, their feet skidding against the ground as they were pushed backward.

"Everly!" I yelled as I jumped over the wall of fire.

She lowered the flames to let me enter before building them back up again to trap us inside. The flames broke off, separating the others from their leader and me.

I moved my blade forward again, ripping through skin, before quickly pulling it back. The vampire looked down at the long slash across his chest and then growled as we locked eyes. His icy blue irises took on a neon glow, and the cut in his skin healed almost as soon as the blade slid across his chest. I had fought many vampires in my time, but none had ever healed that quickly.

My hesitation was all he needed, and within a few long strides, he was standing before me. His hand clasped mine and squeezed. I dropped my katana as he yanked my arm back and spun me around. My back to his chest, he pushed me up against him, lifting my body until his mouth reached my throat. He dug his fingers into my skin. I winced as his short nails drew blood, and I threw my head back. He dropped me as my skull smashed into his nose, and I somersaulted to safety behind the flames.

"Torch 'em," I said, returning to my feet, my katana at my side, and Everly strengthened the fire as Nina encircled them in a shield of air, containing the flames. The fire thickened and rose until we couldn't see them. Blood trickled down my arms, and I ignored the overwhelming desire to tend to my wounds.

I waited. I kept my eyes on the flames, staring at the fire's orange center until I knew there was no possible way they were still alive. I nodded once, and Everly and Nina called upon their elements. The fire quickly disappeared; the ground beneath it was black, charred, dead.

Four vampires stood in the center, unharmed. An iridescent glow surrounded them. They stood upon lush, green grass. The woman smiled knowingly, her blades now in her hands. Their leader still stood before them, but my eyes were drawn to the vampire beside him. His gray eyes took on an eerie glow, turning neon beside his dark skin. His arm was stretched out, his fingertips lightly touching the shimmery wall around them. He closed his hand and drew his arm back. The shimmer followed his command, and the wall disappeared.

I took a predatory stance.

My heart thudded against my chest, and my breathing came in quick bursts. I twirled my katana before me as I took a few steps forward. The blonde dashed from behind her leader, drew her weapon, and brought it down on me. The clank of metal on metal radiated through my arms and down my spine. She pushed her blade against mine, and I fell to my knees. Sweat dribbled down my forehead; I kept my eyes locked on hers. I briefly thought about the other vampires and my cousins.

I let out a loud groan as she took a step forward and put her entire upper body strength against our blades. Under the weight, the blade on my katana snapped,

16

falling to the ground in pieces. I felt the tip of her weapon tease the throbbing vein in my neck. She smiled, and I called upon spirit.

My element surged through me, and as it sparked from my fingertips, I said, "*Incendia!*" The word escaped my lips in a whisper, but it was enough to call upon fire. She screamed, falling backward as she was engulfed in flames.

Spirit gave me a small affinity for each element, and it was enough to distract a vampire. But not enough to inflict real harm. In her fear, she dropped her weapon. I dug my nails into the dirt as I grabbed the handle. I quickly brought it down, digging into her neck.

Her leader flashed before my eyes in a blur, slamming into me. We fell to the ground, but I tightened my grip on the weapon. If I was going to die tonight, I was taking someone with me. I brought my arm back and sank the blade into his gut. His fangs lowered as he groaned. In a daring move, his hand left my arm, grabbed onto the knife, and pulled it out. I wiggled over, bringing my knee up in a sharp jab. He faltered, and I escaped him, somersaulting away and jumping to my feet with knife in hand.

I looked from vampire to vampire: the leader was just getting to his feet, and I knew I needed to kill him quickly. He was the strongest and the biggest threat.

I tossed the knife in the air, grabbed the tip of the blade as it came falling back down, and threw it. It spun as it flew through the air just before sinking into the vampire's chest. His eyes widened in surprise. I ran forward and pulled the knife from his chest as he fell. The female vampire was still on the ground, rubbing her hands over her burnt arms, eyes wide with fear. I threw the knife at her; it landed in her chest but missed her heart. I cursed under my breath but left the knife behind.

The other two vampires had my cousins cornered. They were distracted by Everly and her fire. Nina stood beside her, desperately trying to control the flames so that they too weren't taken. I skidded to a stop behind the one I believed to be the newborn vampire. His Army look-a-like friend turned as I made my move, as if he somehow knew what I was going to do before I even decided. My hands wrapped around the newborn's neck, and with a rough twist, bones snapped. He fell to the ground. Breaking his neck would only offer me limited time before he healed and woke again, but I hoped it was enough.

Three down. One to go. I was impressed with my numbers.

The vampire bared fangs and lunged forward. I jumped to the side, and he grazed past me. In a move too fast for my human eyes, the vampire spun around, grabbed the loose strands from my bun, and yanked my head backward. I cried out.

Before I could call upon my element, before Everly could protect me with her fire, the vampire sank his fangs into my neck.

He viciously tore through skin, my screams echoing through the forest. We weren't far from my coven's sleeping quarters; I hoped someone had heard me. The thought gave me peace. At least someone would come for them. My cousins wouldn't die with me today. I scratched at his hands, but it was no use. He was too strong.

"Enough!" someone yelled.

I blinked away the tears that blurred my vision. Their leader stood before us, the blonde vampire by his side. They both showed no wounds. My breath caught in my throat. How was that possible?

"We're leaving," he added. The vampire's hand squeezed, pulling my hair tighter, and he dropped me. Before I was able to react, they disappeared into the forest. I stared at the trees, at the darkness.

"Stay behind the fire," I said. My throat was coarse. It hurt to speak. It hurt to move. Somewhere in the fight, I had broken ribs, and with each inhalation, the pain stabbed at my side. I told myself I'd count to thirty before I'd believe they were really gone.

I only made it to ten.

I toppled over and landed on my side, where, thankfully, there were no broken bones. I rolled onto my back. I pressed my hand against my neck; blood gushed down my arm. I was sure it was pooling around me now. My wound was too severe. I knew we wouldn't make it to our healer in time.

Thankfully, my cousins ignored my order, lowered their defenses, and sat by my side.

"Oh my," Nina said. "It's bad. It's really bad." Tears spilled, and I brought a hand up to wipe them away, leaving crimson lines in its wake.

"Stop. We can fix this. We need to chant," Everly said. She grabbed a stick. "Bite down."

I obeyed as she brought her free hand up and placed it over my wound. I closed my eyes, and she chanted, calling upon fire. Heat radiated from her palm, burning into my freshly torn skin. I clenched my jaw, digging my teeth into the wood. Searing pain rippled through me. I screamed through my teeth, sure I was going to break the stick in half.

"Avah, are you okay?" Nina asked. Her voice was soothing. She wiped away my tears and took my hand. Everly stopped chanting, and we formed a circle by linking hands. My wound felt sticky, warm. Her affinity for fire only stopped the bleeding; it alone couldn't heal me. We needed all five elements to save my life.

"Focus. Close your eyes," Everly ordered. I knew she spoke only to calm her own nerves. I knew she thought this was useless. The only way we could call upon all five elements was if I called upon spirit, water, and earth. I was weak—too weak. It was nearly impossible.

But we never gave up.

"*Terra. Air. Ignis. Aqua. Spiritus. Terra. Air. Ignis. Aqua. Spiritus.*"

We spoke in unison. We called upon the gods and their magic. We called to our elements. Spirit came naturally to me, just as fire came to Everly and air came to Nina. But I had to fight harder in my weakened state, and I had to fight quicker. The blood loss would soon consume me, but I was more worried about lurking vampires and their heightened sense of smell.

"*Terra.*"

"*Air.*"

"*Ignis.*"

"*Aqua.*"

"*Spiritus.*"

"*Terra.*"

"*Air.*"

"*Ignis.*"

"*Aqua.*"

"*Spiritus.*"

The elements hit me with a force I had never known. It was stronger than the grip of a vampire. It swirled within me, lingering on my wounds. My neck sizzled, the wetness drying, caking. I opened my eyes as air rushed through my lungs. I took deep breaths and silently thanked the gods for healing me once again.

I sat up, instinctively bringing my hand to my neck. I scratched off the dried blood and looked to my cousins.

They smiled and shook their heads. I knew the marks were gone. I let out the breath I had been holding.

With white knuckles, I held the knife at my side until we reached our house.

"Do we tell anyone?" Nina asked, visibly shaken.

No one had come for us, so I knew no one had heard our screams. Informing them now would put too much burden on the coven. We were too close to my birth rite to let vampires interfere. Eventually, we'd have to tell them, but not until I was sure they could handle it.

It occurred to me that if she hadn't been protected behind Everly's wall of fire, she would have been the first to die. While air is a powerful element, it didn't compare to fire. My cousins needed to learn to protect themselves outside of their gifts—just as I had.

I cursed under my breath. All of my training, and I was still defeated. Why didn't I go look for them? They were long gone now. How had the vampire healed so quickly? Why did his eyes glow? What was the shimmer wall? What were they doing in the clearing if not stalking a kill? But most importantly, why didn't they just kill me? I had never encountered vampires who didn't enjoy the kill. I kicked the dirt at my feet as I opened the gate to our property.

"We tell no one. Not yet."

I needed answers, and I wanted them now.

CHAPTER
TWO

"AVAH, YOU BETTER not still be sleeping!" my mother yelled from downstairs.

I groaned and sat on the edge of my bed. I sank my face into the palms of my hands, resting my elbows on my thighs, running my fingers through my matted hair.

"I can do this." My voice was soft, unsure. I had been mentally preparing myself for this day ever since I had discovered I was the next chosen one. I had made it clear to everyone (and to myself) that I would not let it kill me, that they could count on me to end this war.

With one last, quick exhalation, I rose and walked into my bathroom. My muscles were stiff from last night's fight, and even though I had taken a shower immediately after getting home, I knew another would help to clear my mind and soften the tightness. I watched the water swirl down the shower drain, as if I could be hypnotized into a better place. A beach, perhaps? I smiled and called upon spirit. As I closed my eyes, I imagined the grains of sand beneath my feet. The air was heavy with mist and a hint of salt. Seagulls flocked in the distance. My toes burrowed as I walked farther. I kept walking until waves splashed at my heels.

"You're *still* in the shower?" someone said, and I pulled out of my projection.

My breath caught, and I rested my palms against the wall to support my weight. Looking over, I caught a glimpse of long, red locks before the door slammed shut. Shaking my head, I watched the water pool at my feet and let my pulse settle. Pulling out of a projection too quickly left side effects that lasted for days, and today was too important. I needed to stay focused, strong. I jumped out of the shower and rushed through my morning routine. Dashing downstairs, I was greeted by the rest of my coven.

"Nice of you to join us," Nina said.

"Nice of you to knock," I shot back. She sat on the couch with her twin sister by her side. They took their twinness to the extreme and were often adorned in matching outfits and hairstyles. Today, they were wearing yoga pants and tank tops, and their red, curly hair was tied back in thick ponytails. I was sure their relaxed attitude was a show for our coven. We still hadn't spoken about the night before, and had they brought it up then, we would have had to sit through a way-too-long lecture from our high priestess, my mother. But more importantly, the coven would forbid us from patrolling. Mother would argue that, as the chosen one, my safety was more important than my patrolling. She'd send others in my stead, and I couldn't find answers while locked away. My cousins feigned interest in what my aunt was preparing at the dining table.

We often prepared large meals beforehand because rituals tended to drain our energy. It was essential to refuel immediately afterward. I had been forewarned that I wouldn't be able to tap into The Power until I learned to truly control it, but since all chosen witches before me died, no one actually knew how to master it. When Mother received a vision that I was the next chosen one, my coven said I would be all right, that if anyone could control it, it would be me. I had learned astral projection early on, a skill that supposedly took decades to master, so I believed them. I suppressed any reservations. I had to master The Power because there was no other choice.

For today's ritual, my birth rite, they were cooking a feast. Apparently, I needed to refuel more than ever before. Mother had said that she would practice little things with me every day until I was able to harness The Power to kill a vampire. She had explained that I would be able to use very little of The Power for the next couple weeks, since rituals already took too much of a toll on our mortal bodies. I had hoped it wouldn't really take that long.

"Good morning, Avah!" Mother said as she walked into the kitchen from the hallway that led to our preparatory room. She planted a kiss atop my head. "I hope you slept well."

Being chosen was supposed to be an honor, but it felt as though the family of the chosen received the highest respect. Because they would survive. They would be able to benefit from the fruits of the chosen's labor. More importantly, they would be left behind to clean up the mess and rebuild the world. I was the first chosen from our coven. When Mother received the vision from the gods, informing her that the previous witch had failed and that I would take his place come the next full moon, I considered fighting it. Running away. Changing my name, appearance. Marrying a farmer and living my life in seclusion. But reality left me raw. I couldn't betray my coven, even if it sometimes felt as though they were betraying me.

I smiled to reassure her that I was fine and grabbed a bagel, ripping off small chunks. I devoured it quickly, watching the remaining members of my coven scurry around like mice. Each had a job: prepare the meal, prepare the offering, prepare the prep room, prepare the ritual space, and of course, prepare the chosen one. Since our coven had never experienced a birth rite, we treated this ritual as we treated others and hoped it would suffice.

"I think I have everything set for tonight," Mother said. She ran her fingers through my hair and gave me a small smile. A knot formed in my throat as I scanned the ingredients lining our counter. Crystals and herbs cluttered every corner. The air hung heavily between us. As our high priestess, she had to remain strong, for the sake of her coven, but as she was also my mother, I wished I could have opened up to her about my destiny without listening to a lecture on how I should be proud that the gods chose me when there were many other witches who wished for the chance to hold such power, such responsibility. Now, her confidence was gone. Her eyes were pink, puffy. Was she sad I was chosen? Or was she sad because I wasn't ready? I didn't want to know.

Without a word, I nodded and walked down the long hallway. I glanced outside, noticing the thin layer of frost coating the ground. My family had moved to Shasta when I was young. It wasn't the California I was expecting, and even though at times it reminded me of home, I still really missed the snow-filled winters in Wisconsin. I missed the familiar crunch of snow beneath my feet.

At the end of the hall, I stepped into a small room, closing the door behind me. I inhaled deeply as I walked through a cloud of sage. During each Esbat, my mother was sure to cleanse our ritual room, leaving fresh sage burning all night. The smell was overwhelming to some, but I loved it. It felt empowering. It felt… like home.

My mother had dressed the room just as she did for every other Sabbat: while the air was filled with sage, rose petals and mint leaves trailed on the floor against the walls. A claw-foot bathtub sat in the center of the room. I ran my fingers through the steaming water. Peeling my clothes off, I neatly piled them atop a corner stool. Despite the room's warmth, I shivered before climbing into the tub.

The water's magic seeped into my skin. Lying back, I closed my eyes and began to open my chakras, one by one. Beginning with my root chakra, I rubbed the tips of my index fingers with my thumbs, concentrating on the thin layer of water flowing between them. I imagined myself being connected to Mother Earth, her power flowing through me, giving me strength to survive the coming hours.

I focused on my sacral chakra. My left hand gently caressed my right as I focused on my Sacral bone. I continued my cleansing by opening my naval chakra. Raising my arms, I placed my hands just below my solar plexus, letting my fingers intertwine. I focused on my naval opening, allowing the bath to heal my inner turmoil. I stopped for a moment, letting myself inhale deeply, but kept my eyes closed. The sage's smoke flowed through me.

My heart chakra was by far the hardest to open when lying in a bathtub, but once I managed to cross my legs without breaking connection, I lowered my left hand to my knee and my right to just below my breast bone. I smiled when I felt the familiar inner tingling.

I quickly moved on to my throat chakra. I often had difficulties speaking what was on my mind, so I wasn't surprised that this chakra was the most difficult to open. After imagining the constricted muscles moving freely, I was able to easily move onto my third eye.

As a spirit user, I'd always been able to open and re-close my third eye with ease. I enjoyed the momentary bliss it brought me, but leaving your third eye open too long risked *touching* spirits who might be lingering in The Beyond, the space between life and death. Although I wouldn't mind the conversation, I didn't have the time to take on any extra *projects* my new friends might bring with them. Visiting The Beyond was considered taboo because of its formidable addictions, so I hadn't told anyone that I'd perfected that ability early on.

My first encounter with The Beyond was while dreaming. I learned at an early age that my affinity for spirit allowed me to possess the power to astral project, a rare and coveted gift that allowed my spiritual being to leave my physical one.

Enjoying my hazy surroundings, I began to pull back, leaving The Beyond. I compelled my third eye to close. With my chakras cleansed and closed, I soaked in the spelled water. I focused on today's ritual, trying to ignore the fight from last night. I would soon become the most powerful witch in the world, but I still felt vulnerable. I wanted answers; I wanted to feel safe again. I needed to find the vampires from last night. I shook my head with hope that it would also shake away the desire to look into last night's events. I needed to stay focused. I told myself that I would not think about those vampires for the rest of the night.

My mother entered the room dressed in a burgundy cloak, traditional Pagan attire for such rituals. My aunt followed, dressed to match, hands folded at her naval holding my cloak, and the door closed behind them. My mother carried the burning bundle of sage that rested on the adjacent altar and waved it back and forth, cleansing my aunt's aura. When my mother finished smudging my aunt, she handed the bundle of sage to her sister. My aunt then mimicked my mother's actions, cleansing her aura. Cleansing was essential to our rituals. One could never enter the circle with negative energy.

My preparation was coming to an end, but it felt as though I had just begun my cleansing. Experience had taught me that even when it felt like only minutes had passed, chances were, hours had flown by. I thanked the gods for our spelled tub, which kept the water steaming.

"Stand, my child," Mother said. Tonight, she was no longer my mother. She was my high priestess, and I was a tool of the gods.

And with those few words, she helped me step out of the tub. My throat knotted, and bile forced its way into my mouth. I swallowed it down and ignored the goose bumps that formed as I left the warm water. She covered my naked body with my cloak. While my mother buttoned the front, my aunt stepped behind me, placing a bowl of dried rose petals in my hand. My aunt wrapped my hair in a long braid, and I handed her petal after petal as she stuck the pieces of flower in my hair. I closed my eyes and pretended I was a princess awaiting the arrival of her prince. My heart burned at the realization that I wanted that fantasy more than my magical reality.

"It's time," my mother said as she placed her hands

on my arms and rubbed. My goose bumps began to fade. I nodded.

Turning on her heel, she led us out of the room. I looked out the window as we passed. Those in our coven without magic continued on with their evening. They knew of the importance of this day, but it played little role in their daily lives. Without magic, there was no place for them in our ritual, so only thirteen would participate: besides my mother, aunt, and me, ten others awaited our entrance, including my aunt's daughters, Nina and Everly. They had already begun entering our circle.

We stepped onto the back porch; farther out, I could see that our circle of witches was perfectly illuminated by moonlight. The forest outlined the clearing and left just enough sky for us to admire the full moon and stars.

Leaving my side, my mother and aunt entered the circle. Slowly, I crept my way toward the members of my coven, most being members by blood. My mother stood at the head of the circle, my aunt took her place at my mother's right side, and beside her, my cousins stood. Eight others, men and women, completed the circle, leaving only the center open. Watching their lips move, I couldn't hear their chant. I looked out into the woods as I approached the circle, my goose bumps returning as the breeze increased.

"How do you enter?" Mother asked, holding the tip of an athamé to my throat.

"With perfect love and perfect trust," I replied.

She lowered the blade and stepped aside. I entered the circle and stood directly in the crosshairs of twelve powerful witches.

My mother shouted several Latin incantations. As the chanting grew louder, the twist in my stomach grew tighter. Mirroring the members of my coven, I held my arms out to my sides, palms facing the full moon. Looking into the dark sky, I squeezed my eyes shut.

I wasn't sure what to expect. Being one of only three spirit users in my coven, I often had a major role to play, but during this ritual, my mother had directed me to do nothing but remain willing. I had wondered if her lack of explanation was because she too wasn't sure of what to expect.

The air became moist, hot. A film developed on my skin, dripping down the crevices of my body. My head was spinning, my eyes closed. I felt as though I was falling, but I refused to break connection. I would not cry for help, for mercy. My coven continued calling their elements, making it more difficult to breathe as each moment passed. Their chants grew louder, and my world continued to spin until, suddenly, it stopped.

The Power hit me in waves, entering through my crown chakra and making its way down my spine until it touched every part of my being. The layers unfolded within, forcing their will upon me, and I welcomed their smooth caress. Splattering into the deep crevices of my soul, The Power took hold of my spirit; my astral self rose above the physical world, smiling down at the beautiful wreckage it left behind. My astral self flowed back into my mortal shell. My skin felt binding, tight, as if it could no longer hold such power.

My legs buckled beneath me, unable to hold my weight. I landed on my side and rolled onto my back. Briefly, muscle spasms made it difficult to breathe. I opened my eyes. The members of my coven remained in their places and continued chanting.

I gazed back up at the moon, hoping it could give me the strength I'd need to control The Power that burned within me.

My muscles relaxed, and I began to feel the soothing effects of The Power. As it seeped into every fiber of my body, my mind began to cloud. My eyelids became heavy; I fought to maintain consciousness. I felt as if I was connected to the ground that held my body. Each blade of grass tickled my skin. Mountain air tingled in my lungs. Moonlight cast a glow around my frame.

Nausea boiled in my gut and burned its way into my mouth. I rolled over and heaved in the center of circle. I spit the last bit on the ground and looked to my mother. I was embarrassed. I had let my physical fear control my body. My mother stood directly before me, but she looked into the distance, jaw open, eyes wide with fear.

Still on all fours, I glanced backward. My eyes didn't have time to adjust to the darkness of the woods before they approached.

Vampires.

Instinctively, my coven began slowly backing away, but my mother stepped forward. The witches formed a line and intertwined fingers.

Still unable to move, I cursed under my breath. Where I lay, I was in front of their line, unprotected, and only a few feet from the demons. These weren't the vampires from last night, but I believed they were sent by them. Briefly, I wondered if telling Mother of our encounter with the vampires would have prevented another attack, but I shook my head at the thought. I couldn't distract myself with should haves and could haves. I couldn't change the past. I could only save the future. Our ritual was successful. I could feel The Power within me, and I had to protect my coven.

"Let's get inside, Tatiana," my aunt said.

"I will not leave her." Mother didn't need to look where I lay. I knew she spoke of me. She wouldn't leave me. No, she *couldn't* leave me. As our high priestess, it was her duty. Protect each member of the coven at all costs—regardless of the weight the decision inflicted.

"Go inside," I said, my breath barely above a hush. I pushed myself off the ground, but I only succeeded in becoming dizzier. My legs wobbled. I could feel The Power flowing through my veins, yet it was just out of reach when I tried to tap into it. I didn't understand. Wasn't this why I was chosen? Where was my strength? Suddenly, I panicked. Where was my katana? A broken blade was better than none at all.

My mother took a step forward, and the vampires

made their move. We knew of the darkness that lurked in the night, and Mother had always anticipated vampires would find our home. During every full moon, when elemental magic was at its most powerful, our coven spelled a protective wall around our sleeping quarters. It was tied to the full moon, and as each new full moon surfaced, the spell needed to be recast. Because of my calling, we hadn't completed the protection spell yet. It would take mere minutes for the vampires to tear through our weakened defenses.

Consumed by rage and without options, I willed myself strength from the moon. I threw my arms to the sky, shouted a Latin incantation, and sucked the moon's energy into me. Its power showered down upon us, soaking into my body. My mother reached my side.

I stood and threw my arms out in front of me and watched as the ground gave way; a deep crevice that ended in blackness formed, separating them from us. I called upon earth, and earth obeyed. I matched their strength and tore through limbs as I called upon air; its newly razor-sharp edges eagerly did my bidding. My skin sizzled as a few vampires combusted before my eyes. I called upon fire, feeling its heat radiate through me.

"Avah! Stop!" Mother cried out, grabbing onto my arm.

I watched as she aged before me. Her smooth skin turned to wrinkles; her eyes turned dark and sunken.

Shocked, I dropped my arms and released the moon and witches I had imprisoned in my power-fueled rage. The Earth's energy rejuvenated those before me, and the vampires attacked before I had time to stop them.

A vampire stood before me, clenching my neck beneath its cool hand, and without hesitation, it crushed my throat and tossed my frail body to the ground. My mother screamed my name as I gasped for air. In heavy, uneven breaths, I asked Mother Earth to heal me. I reached within myself, begging The Power to save my soul.

As my eyelids began to close, I watched a glistening blade slide across the throat of a vampire. His body collapsed to the ground, his head rolling to the side. Behind him, shadow figures stepped out of the darkness. A new group of vampires emerged from the woods. Our coven's saviors hacked through our enemy with simple twists and turns of their weapons.

Vampires. The vampires I had encountered and

failed to kill. But the newcomers fought on the side of witches. Ripping the fiends off members of my coven, they defeated our enemies and carried our wounded into the safety of our home.

As my soul slipped into The Beyond, I felt at peace. My pain diminished. The breath I begged for flowed within me. I smiled as I sank deeper into darkness.

"Look at me," he said. "Focus." His voice was smooth and echoed in my head. His words twisted around me, lifting me to him, to this world of agony. Torn away from my blissful darkness, I opened my eyes. His icy blue irises stared back at me.

He knelt on the ground before me, holding my bruised body against his. My head, too heavy for me to lift, was supported by his other hand. Only inches away from my face, his breath was hot on my cheek, his hand cool on my back. His aura burned brightly before me, pushing against my own. Momentarily, I was able to let go of the pain that encompassed my soul and grab onto his essence.

He tipped my head back, opening my mouth. He pressed against me, raising a hand. His irises brightened into the same neon glow as the night before. A rusted substance dripped into my open mouth as his lips grazed against mine. His essence, his power, soared through me, healing wounds as it passed. He reached The Power that was nestled deeply within me, and I could sense the vampire fighting to maintain his hold on my life. A force expelled him from my body, taking his healing powers with him.

Tearing my watery eyes from his, I searched for my mother in the midst of a war. The vampires helped my coven, but they couldn't save everyone. Bodies scattered the sacred ground of our ritual. Witches. Vampires. Their fragmented bits looked eerily identical in the moonlit patches.

I watched my cousins fight a pair of ruthless vampires. Their long red hair whipped behind them with each abrupt turn. My aunt called upon air and sliced through each vampire she passed as she slowly reached her daughters.

Staring once again into his eyes, the world melted around me. My breathing became heavy, and my sputtering heart made it hard to focus. I would not fail my coven. I would not leave them unprotected.

The pain subsided, and in a last desperate attempt to

survive, I begged, "Save me," knowing that there was only one way he knew how. My grip on life was weakening, and in my most desperate of times, I saw my reprieve in his eyes. As life slipped through my grasp, I panicked. I would give anything to survive my birth rite, to protect my coven—even if the only thing I could offer was my mortality.

I whimpered and scratched at his body as his fangs lengthened into two bloodthirsty points.

His blue irises took on an eerie glow as he allowed the demon within him to surface. I turned my head, exposing my unmarked neck.

I glanced at the world around me. The remaining members of my coven fought to control their magic against the vampires. Against what I was to become. Yet, the vampire holding me looked different than the murderous eyes around us. The animals surrounding us were just that: animals. Their dirty hair and blood-stained bodies contained the souls of fiends.

I gasped as my neck was pierced, my nails digging into his arms, marking him in the same way he had marked me the night before. After mere moments of pain, I was wrapped in a blanket of pure bliss. I slid my hand up his strong, muscular arms, tangling my fingers in his thick brown hair. Briefly, I forgot the world around us. I forgot the war. I forgot my hatred. I forgot death.

There was only him.

There was only me.

There was only blood.

Almost as soon as it began, he pulled away, ignoring my unconvincing protests as I tried to pull him back to me. In one swift motion, he bit into his skin and placed his dripping wrist to my lips. Unable to control myself, I grabbed onto him and drank as though it were the only source of water in the midst of a desert.

My eyes became heavy, my body weak. I fell limp in his arms. I held on to sound, to his scent. With each breath, my heart pounded in my head, and I lost all emotion. I didn't care what happened to me, to my coven, to my savior. I just wanted the darkness, the need that was nestled in the pit of my stomach.

He pushed through the coven's protective wall, carried me upstairs, and gently rested me on my bed. Brushing the hair away from my eyes, he said, "You'll need to feed when you awaken. Don't wait. The hunger will consume you if you give it the chance."

I reached for him, brushing my fingers against his cool cheek. His hand grabbed mine, and pain flashed behind those icy blue eyes. As I opened my mouth to thank him, words were just out of reach, but darkness was there to consume me.

CHAPTER
THREE

YOU NEED TO *wake up, Avah.*

My mother's voice echoed in my mind. She stood before me, slowly backing away. The light followed her exit. I thrashed and pleaded for an escape, fearing the inevitable darkness she'd leave behind. The air was hazy, thick. I fought to breathe, to stay awake.

Mother? I said, unable to hide the fear in my voice. My word echoed. I felt trapped in my own skin. Though I saw nothing, I knew time stood still. I could *feel* it. The darkness of eternity.

I ran toward her, grabbing onto the flowing, sheer-white gown. My fingers fell numb, unable to grip as the fabric slipped through.

Please don't leave me, I said.

The shadows moved closer, circling me. I whipped around, lashing back and forth. Her silhouette slowly began to fade. It was consuming her, just as I knew it would come for me, too. I backed away, but with each step, it moved closer.

My lungs filled with the misty air, and I fell to my knees, hacking. I was drowning, drowning without water. The darkness, the air, the haze, it consumed me, stealing away my breath, forcing me to my knees, to beg for life.

Avah, she said, and I looked up, my chest heaving. *Wake up.* She spoke, yet her lips never moved. I reached out to her, but my limb fell numb, hitting the ground in a thump. I slumped over, unable to hold my own weight. My breath came in short bursts. I was dying. I looked to her as I accepted my fate. She gave me one final glance before smiling and fading into darkness. And I was left alone in The Beyond.

"You need to leave." My aunt's voice squeaked under her threatening tone. Darkness still surrounded me, but the familiar scent of my home crept its way in. I inhaled deeply. Sage.

"She'll awaken soon," another voice said. It was the vampire. The one I'd fought in the clearing, the one

48

who'd tried to save me after the ritual. Inside, I fought to awaken, to stand, to scream, to do anything, *something*. But I couldn't. I was trapped inside my body, an unyielding shell that refused to give way.

"And when she does, we'll send her on her way. You're *all* not welcome here," Everly replied. My heart seemed to sink into the pit of my stomach.

"Relax," another voice said. "We won't bite." I cringed at the vampire's joke. I imagined him with a sly smile. He thought he was funny. I thought my blade would slide through him like a knife in butter.

My eyes shot open; my back arched as my muscles spasmed, and I let out an uncontrollable screech that nearly shook the house to its foundation. My muscles tensed, and I flopped off the bed and onto the floor like a fish in search of water. My chest cringed. I felt different. Lighter.

The door was flung open, and a blue-eyed vampire stared back at me. He slowly walked into the room as I crawled into a predator stance. Time seemed to slow as he approached. Digging my nails into the floor boards, I growled as blood trickled around my fingertips. He took another step toward me, his scent following. He smelled of musk and blood.

Several figures crowded around the vampire. I felt a drip of drool dribble down my chin as the scent from my bloody fingertips reached my nose. The air was thick and heavy; the scent lingered around me, causing my stomach to grumble. Eyes widened around me.

"You should leave," the blue-eyed vampire said.

Fangs exposed, I lunged at my attacker. I crushed the vampire's neck with a slight squeeze of my hand, tossing his limp body aside, and reached for the next closest thing: a witch. I knew it was wrong. I knew I didn't want to hurt her. But I couldn't stop. My hunger was in control the moment I willingly relinquished my mortality.

"Stop!" she yelled as I was thrown backward. I flew across the room and slammed into the far wall; framed pictures shattered on the floor beside me.

I jumped to my feet and was met by another witch. Her stretched-out arm was all that separated the distance between us. She drew her index and middle fingers out as a warrior would draw a sword upon his enemies. I smiled and inhaled deeply, licking my lips. She smelled of herbs. She smelled clean. She smelled like food.

"Please don't make me hurt you, Avah," she said.

"Listen to my voice. You can fight this." She didn't know. She didn't understand. I didn't want to hurt her, but hunger boiled like acid in my gut. It stung; it squeezed my innards until there was nothing but goo.

My brows furrowed as I released another, powerful growl, and the animal within left me no choice. I took a step forward, and the witch yanked her fingers into her palm before instantly throwing them out again. I was hit with a powerful force that pinned me to the wall.

Spirit.

The blue-eyed vampire stepped before me, grabbing my arms and slamming my body against the wall. My head thrashed as I faced him. Why wasn't he dead? I had crushed his spine when I took his neck. Confused, I looked to his throat. It bore no mark of my fingers. Instead, it revealed a thick, protruding vein. A gasp escaped my nearly sealed lips. My fangs lengthened, and my body loosened.

"Control your hunger," he said. He relaxed his grip, and I fell into him. I ran my fingers through his hair and buried my nose into the crevice of his neck. "We will soon feed."

"Jasik, don't," a voice from behind said. I felt his

heart puttering within his chest, forcing blood to pump faster inside his veins. I gripped his t-shirt in my free hand and groaned slightly as I placed the tips of my fangs against his skin. He leaned into me, running his hand down the arch of my back. "Fight it," the voice added.

Irritated, I glanced toward the speaker. The three vampires stood just steps away, enclosing me in a threshold of steel. Dressed to fight, each was armed with knives, their leather attire expressing their solid definition. They were the same vampires I had fought in the field.

"Jasik, fight it!" the vampire yelled, emphasizing each word.

I yanked him back as he tried to slowly pull away. He was powerless beneath my grip; the control I had over his life made me euphoric. His eyes met mine. In a swift motion, he twisted my arms around, releasing himself from my grasp, and stepped back. He quickly spun me around, and I faced a cornered, full-length mirror.

"You mustn't lose yourself to the hunger," Jasik whispered, his breath hot against my ear.

A pang of desire crept through my body as I examined his closeness in our reflection. I pushed it down, disgusted.

"Look," he said, his breath tickling my earlobe.

I obeyed, admiring my figure in the mirror: My brown hair fell raggedly to my shoulders; my frame was toned and defined, my complexion clear and pale. My eyes bore no resemblance to their once plain, dark-brown color. Instead, a set of violet irises stared back at me.

He released his grip, and I reluctantly walked to the mirror and placed my palms and the tip of my nose against the glass. The girl who stood before me was no one who I recognized. Through lacy puffs of steam, I watched her figure disappear and reappear before my eyes as my hot breath clouded the reflection in the mirror.

"What *is* she?" Nina asked.

I whipped around, annoyed at her tone. I ignored the snide comment and looked past my visitors. A cluttered desk sat in the corner. Yellowed photos and rusted medals sat atop the chipped wood table. Bundles of crumpled clothes were piled on the floor, and a sheet-less bed lined the far wall. Everything about the room felt familiar, yet foreign. As if I didn't belong in the place that I'd called home for so long.

Bile crept its way into my throat, and I swallowed hard to keep it down. I remembered everything from the night before. I had asked the blue-eyed vampire to save my life by changing me. I remembered the fight, my fear. And then it all came rushing back.

"Avah, we have to go," Jasik said, extending his hand. I looked from his eyes to his hand. Had he lost his mind? Why would I ever go with him?

"Were there casualties?" I asked, ignoring the vampire and looking to my mother. I ignored the overwhelming sensation to rip her throat open. I squeezed my palms shut and focused on the pain in my hands rather than the one in my gut.

"Yes, and they were severe," she replied slowly. Her eyes trailed down my body. She looked... distant. Unsure. Afraid. Afraid of me, her daughter, of what I had become.

It pained me to see her so hesitant of her own flesh and blood. *Blood.* My breath caught as the sound of her blood moving through her veins overpowered me. I licked my lips and closed my eyes. Breathe. Focus on your breathing. In and out. A hand grabbed onto mine, and I opened my eyes, smiling as I hoped to find my mother beside me, trusting that I would not betray her.

He was there. Looking down at me. His lips in a hard line as he forced a fake smile. I ripped my hand from his before quickly bringing it up again and thrusting it against his chest. He flew backward with the ease of a feather blowing in the wind. My jaw dropped, and I looked down to my hands. They seemed foreign. The lines of my palm looked different. My fingers were thinner, my nails thicker.

"Don't touch me!" I yelled as he stood, dusting off the chunks of plaster that had fallen onto his chest.

"Avah, I promise I'm not going to hurt you."

His words sounded sincere. Every fiber of my being wanted to trust him, to take his hand, to believe that I would be okay. But I knew the truth. I was a vampire now. There would never be an okay. My coven would disown me. No one would ever allow it. The gods had probably already sent a vision to another spirit user to replace me after I had...

I had failed them. Tears burned behind my eyes and threatened to spill. How could I give up so easily? I had failed my coven the moment I had received The Power. I had failed every single witch by practically begging the vampire to make me immortal. I would now be hunted by those I had fought so hard to protect.

"You must feed." His words made me shudder. *You must feed.* He reached out his hand again. "It's okay," he whispered as if only he and I were in the room.

His eyes, like his tone, were sincere. It made me sick to think it, but I knew he cared for me. I knew he wanted to protect me. I didn't understand why.

Part of my training was to study the vampire species through the eyes of humans, so I knew popular movies and television shows often represented vampires in a unique light. A specific characteristic always stood out as the foulest one.

Sire bond.

Had we been bonded? What did that even mean? I shook away the thought and looked to my coven. My mother, aunt, and two cousins were standing before me, but I saw no one else.

I swallowed hard as a tear slid down my cheek. I knew they hated me. I could see it in their eyes. They reeked of fear. But I needed to know. "Everyone else, they're gone, aren't they?" I nodded as I said my last few words. I knew the answer. If they weren't standing before me now, then they were either casualties in the war or severely wounded and brought to our healer.

"Only three others survived the attack," my mother said. She sounded different. Colder. Her uncertainty was gone. I knew I was to blame.

I thought back to my hours of preparation and to the ritual. I knew then, deep down, I *knew* the vampires were there, watching, waiting, in the woods. I felt them. They were close enough to make me vomit during the ritual. I had stupidly tossed my feelings aside as nerves, but in reality, they were symptoms warning me of the impending doom.

"Avah Taylor," Mother said, her voice quivering, tears forming behind her eyes. I knew she was to pass down sentencing. Regardless of whether or not a witch chose to be a vampire, she was given the same sentence: death.

I stood tall. I accepted my sentence. I would have died for my coven.

"I hereby relinquish your duty to this coven. You are no longer a member nor are you family. Due to your previous status in this coven, I will grant you five minutes. Gather your things and leave."

I nodded as tears fell. She could not sentence me to death. I knew that choice would bear heavily on her later.

"Should you not be gone when your time runs out," she continued, "we will release our full power on you."

She stopped. I waited for her to finish, but she said nothing. I knew she couldn't; she couldn't actually say it, that she'd *kill* me, her daughter, the chosen one.

The witches around her tensed. I wondered if they too worried that she would order them to kill me. I wondered if they wanted to. To them, I was no longer family. I was the threat.

I said nothing as I turned and faced my things. My pictures were a shattered mess on the floor. My books from classes I had taken at our local college were in stacks on my desk. Dirty and clean clothes were piled on the floor. What was I to take? My coven. Could I take my coven?

No, I couldn't. They didn't want me anymore. I was hurt by their reaction and ashamed of my decision to so easily accept this new fate. But stubbornness left me in silence.

The vampire offered me his hand again. His eyes

beckoned to me, as if he were silently asking me to trust him. Looking from his eyes to his hand, I opted for the only option I was given and took his peace offering. With his hand held in mine, we left my room, and my family, behind.

The air outside was refreshing. I begged for it to blow away the fear, the doubt, the pain that clouded my mind. With the slightest inhalation, I was discovering new scents. From flowers to meat and rust to salt, I smelled the world as if life was sprawled on a platter before me. But more than that, I could *feel* it. The life that drove nature to survive flowed through me. It was as if I could tap into its energy and harness its power as my own.

"You show an impressive level of control I've yet to see in a newborn," the vampire said.

I yanked my hand from his and wrapped my arms around my chest. I didn't like my decision to simply leave my coven behind, but I hated my choice to leave with *them*.

"I'm Jasik."

I rolled my eyes and looked away. I mentally told myself that I had no choice. If I stayed behind, my family would kill me. If I left with the vampires, then maybe, just maybe, I could learn to control what I was, and my coven would welcome me back. I could become the ultimate tool.

Being a chosen-one-turned-vampire had to have its perks.

"We need to get back. The sun will rise in a few hours," another vampire said.

He glanced at me, jaw clenched. His eyes were bright green, and they seemed to outline each curve of my body as his gaze dropped down. I felt vulnerable under his stare. He didn't look at me with wonder, curiosity, or lust. He looked at me with disgust, hatred, and fear. He quickly turned away and joined the others. I felt odd beside the blue-eyed vampire: vulnerable yet safe. My hatred toward him was tinged with curiosity.

"That was Malik, my brother."

I ignored him.

I looked at my house, my eyes lingering on my bedroom window. My mother stood beside the curtain, watching me, before quickly stepping out of view. I wanted to call out to her, beg her to let me stay, but I knew leaving was my only option. They would never be safe around me until I was able to control what I was.

Focusing on the room, I closed my eyes and listened. At first, I heard nothing, but then the world consumed me.

"Stay safe, my love," my mother whispered.

"Can you *believe* Braedon said that?" a girl said with a chuckle. Her voice was distant, hushed. She sounded young, weak.

"Did you want anything from the store?" a man asked. He was closer. His voice was coarse, deep. He was closer to me than the girl. I heard him clearly, as if he stood just behind me. But no one was there.

Laughing.

Crying.

Horns.

Barking.

Clanking heels.

Hiss of a cat.

Squeal of tires.

Sizzling of a fryer.

I dug my fingers into my hair, collapsing to the ground. My mouth opened, but I couldn't breathe.

"Focus on just me," Jasik said as he pulled my head

against his chest. "Shield yourself from the world. You can do it. Raise your shield, Avah."

"I-I can't. It's s-so loud!" I said, pushing myself harder against him and squeezing my eyes shut. I was sure the witches had done something. I had outworn my welcome, and now, they were using their powers against me. This was it; this was the end.

"Avah, you can do this. You're strong. Pull your strength from within. Use it to shield yourself from the world."

"I can't!" I yelled, angry that he was barking out orders I couldn't comprehend.

"Jeremiah! She needs you," he yelled.

I opened my eyes as a hand firmly grasped the back of my head. Kneeling before me, the vampire with dark skin and glowing, gray irises pulled me into his arms. I met his gaze, and slowly, the world went silent.

"She'll be fine," Jeremiah said, dropping his arms. "I'll slowly remove it to make the transition easier." He walked away.

After the pain subsided, I stood. "What did he do to me?"

Jasik's face hardened as he stared at me. "Let's get

somewhere safe, and then we'll talk."

"No. Tell me everything. *No,*" I said, taking several steps backward.

After several minutes, he softened and said, "It's not that simple, Avah."

"Make it simple." I wouldn't budge. I'd sit outside my home until my coven came for us if that's what it took.

"I've never encountered a vampire like you. And I've been around a long time," he said as he turned and began walking toward the others. "I've heard the stories, but I always thought they were just that: stories."

I walked beside him, meeting his gaze. "What do you mean? Why am I so different?" I said. I kicked a stone with my foot, watching it bounce against the concrete, stopping once it reached a patch of grass.

I felt the pavement's vibrations rattle through my body as the stone glided against it. I knew it had to be my status as the chosen one. I had never heard of a witch becoming a vampire, though I always thought it had to have happened over the centuries. Elders must have assumed a witch would one day turn, because they passed down laws and penalties against it. Speaking of turning into an immortal came at a high price. The betrayal to one's coven would cost a witch her life. I wondered if the vampire knew I was chosen to harness The Power of the gods, the power that was to annihilate the vampire race.

Glancing up from the ground, I watched as two teenagers approached us. The boy had his arm around the back of the girl's neck, pulling her close to him. She smiled as he did this, probably enjoying the safety he provided—not realizing that there were monsters in this world that his arm was no match for.

I examined his physique as a scientist would in a laboratory. His arms and chest were tightly bound by his t-shirt. Thin white lines danced across his pale skin. Stretch marks. The closer we came, the more I saw. Goosebumps covered his skin; fine hairs stood on end. I remembered that the air was cool during the ritual, though I didn't feel chilled now. I felt the breeze but not the cold.

They were just feet in front of us. His shirt seemed to become tighter and tighter the closer they came. I wondered if he took steroids. Time seemed to slow as they passed. The wind picked up, blowing their scent into my open and willing nostrils. I licked my lips, my tongue sticking to dry parts of skin.

Shutting my eyes, I swallowed hard as my throat began to close. Its dryness was painful, scratchy. When I opened my eyes again, my fangs were exposed, and I was just steps behind the humans. I hadn't been aware of taking the final steps toward them, and I didn't care. An arm's length was all that separated them from death, from me. Just before I could leap from behind, I was yanked backward.

"No." His voice was stern, controlling. I was shocked that he cared. Vampires were murderers. Why would he stop me?

Looking up, I met his eyes. I didn't understand why he had stopped me, but I was thankful he had. Remembering who I was had become more and more difficult as the night went on. Jasik's proximity felt oddly intimate, making my skin burn. My fangs retracted, and I pulled away from my captor, horrified at my newfound hunger.

I shook my head and wrapped my body in my arms. In that moment, I hadn't cared if I took that teenager's life. I had lost control. I had wanted to kill—I was *ready* to kill. But I didn't *feel* like a killer. I just felt hungry. I dropped my arms and resorted to the only thing I knew how to do in this new world: I ran.

CHAPTER
FOUR

SOMEONE WAS CALLING after me, but the voice quickly grew faint. As I ran through the woods, the forest blurred at my sides. Yet, the world remained clear before me. As my feet pounded against the hard, packed ground, my legs never grew tired. Weary of my strength, I came to an abrupt stop and fell to my knees.

"What have I become?" I said aloud, burying my face in my palms.

"Avah?" a voice said. Footsteps approached from behind.

I jumped to my feet and spun around. I watched the vampires approach me with caution. We were in another small clearing. The forest that surrounded Shasta had often protected me from prying eyes while patrolling. I found comfort in northern California's seclusion.

I knew these woods in the dead of night. I knew where I had hidden weapons, buried deep in the ground. I knew the trails to find home. I knew the berries that grew in the bushes. I knew of the hidden cemetery, where my coven buried our loved ones. These woods were part of my life, my family. I felt sickened when I thought of these vampires using the earth as their hunting grounds.

"Everything will be okay," he said. His words were soothing. I was angry, confused, but as soon as he spoke, I grew calm. His reassurance was all that it took to make me feel at peace, even when only moments before a storm had raged within me. The thought of him having power over me left me sick. I refused to believe he could sway my feelings. "We'll find you something to eat."

I shook my head. "I don't even know what I am anymore. How can that be okay?" His words annoyed me. How was it that the undead thing before me was so optimistic?

"You're like us now. A Hunter," he said. He signaled to the others with his hand, waving them away in some secret movement that I didn't understand, and two of the three ran off into the woods while Malik took several steps toward me, concern filling his eyes.

"But different," I said. I was different. I needed to remember that.

"I'll go with Lillie and Jeremiah. You'll be all right?" Malik said.

Jasik nodded without looking away. "Maybe it's time to have that talk? Malik will make sure they find something, so why don't you sit down and relax."

I obeyed. I was eager to learn more. I needed to understand what I had become. Everything I knew about vampires had been taught to me by witches. Our elders mandated daily gatherings. We had learned how to fight, how to scavenge, how to use our magic as a tool to kill.

We were taught that vampires had always been a feral species, one that was a mystery to witches. We knew they were the cause of almost every human war. Luckily, witches had stepped in before the vampires' existence became known, but in the 40s, witches came close to losing the war against vampires.

One vampire realized his race was close to extinction. In retaliation, he formed an army and murdered over five million humans in Europe. When he knew witches and the human armies were mere moments from trapping him, he took his own life. A coward's way out. My grandmother was a child during these horrific times, and with the rise of each full moon, she would tell us the story of how one vampire had the power to almost annihilate this group of people.

Her stories were powerful tools against the vampire race: they would instill a mindset of murder into the next generation of witches.

"I don't know what you know, so I don't know where to begin," Jasik said, frustration filling his voice.

"How about the beginning?" In truth, I remembered everything I had ever been taught. I remembered my hatred for his kind and the disgust in myself for asking him to change me instead of trusting in myself to control The Power.

"We're supposedly mortal enemies, you know. You and me."

I said nothing. What was I to say? We weren't *supposedly* enemies. There was nothing supposed about it. We were enemies.

"The blood running through your veins isn't just that of a vampire. The witch in you didn't let go when you died. That power is still flowing through you, making you *different.*" *The witch in you didn't let go.* I choked down the snide remark begging to be let loose. He treated my heritage with disrespect, as if being a witch was similar to vampirism. Mortality was nothing like immortality. Witches were *nothing* like vampires.

"What do you mean?" I asked.

"I've heard stories throughout the many long years I've been a vampire. Rumors, mostly, because our lack of an encounter with a being such as yourself has prevented us from proving any real existence of a hybrid creature."

"Hybrid?" I asked, dumbfounded.

"Well, more or less. That would be the appropriate human label, but to us, you're so much more."

"How so?"

"If the myth is true, then you would be the answer to our problems. A feasible way to control the fight, to give us the upper hand."

"What fight?"

"Against Rogue vampires."

"You're fighting vampires?"

"More or less."

"You protect your kind from your kind?"

"You see, vampires have a goddess. Like mortals have their gods. Do you know why the mortals' gods gifted humans with power? To protect humans. Hunters are no different. I guess you could say we're the witches of the vampire race," he said with a chuckle. "So yes, we protect vampires from vampires."

Suddenly, the history I remembered seemed drastically different than the story he was telling. I had been taught that vampires were nothing more than soulless demons inhabiting human-looking bodies. I had been taught that though a vampire may look like your loved one, talk like your loved one, they were not your loved one anymore. The demon had many disguises and used many tricks to buy your trust. But falling for them would cost a witch her life.

"Your gods gave witches powers just like our goddess gave vampires powers. Gifted humans found a new name: witches. Gifted vampires received a new one, too: Hunters. That's what we do. We hunt. We hunt Rogues, vampires too dangerous to live. We protect our kind from those poisoned by power and hatred."

"How do you know which ones shouldn't live?"

"Rogues stand out. They're different—the way they

move, the way they look, the way they think," he said as he rose.

"Jasik... why did you save me?" I blurted the words before I even realized I wanted to ask.

The question sounded stupid as it left my tongue. He had saved me because I begged for it, right? I wasn't so sure that that was his only motive. Why were they there the night before our ritual? He saved me then, too. He saved me from Malik's fangs. Did they know what was to happen the following eve? How did they get to our coven in time? Why did they try to save us? I had so many questions, and I didn't know where to begin.

"We were hunting them. The Rogue vampires that attacked your coven."

As he spoke, his eyes grew distant. I couldn't understand why it affected him as much as it seemed to. I hated that I couldn't understand the connection that now tied us together. But more so, I hated me. I hated my decision to become a vampire. I hated my fear of dying. I hated that I didn't trust The Power. But most importantly, I hated that I didn't hate the vampire before me. I wasn't even afraid of him. Somehow, deep inside, I knew he wouldn't hurt me. And that sickened me. I wanted to despise everything he stood for... but I couldn't. I wondered if turning had changed more of me than I realized.

"Had we been even a minute later, we wouldn't have been able to save you. Any of you. We were informed of a group of Rogues that had been destroying small villages, making their way across the coast, and we were sent to remove the problem."

"And you did, right? *All* of them?" A gnawing in the pit of my gut told me I missed something—an instinctual predatory reaction I began to feel the moment I witnessed the death of my father: kill or be killed. I thought back to the fight. I passed out before it had ended.

"We killed all but a few."

My world came crashing down as the realization hit me hard: the vampires who stole my life from me, the vampires who *forced* me to play the only hand I had been dealt, still walked, still lived, still breathed. Anger boiled within me as an acidic slop rose in my chest. I forced it down in a quick gulp. The thought made me sick, furious. They should be dead. Everyone who had any part in the attack should have perished beside the fallen members of my coven. I would make them pay.

"You were sent? By whom?" The idea of a vampire government and secret militia terrified me more than I would admit—even if I had become one of them.

"Our High Priestess. As Hunters, it is our duty to protect our coven. These Rogues were creating a problem that needed quick resolution."

"I see," I said, trying to wrap my head around the world that thrived when the lights went out. It felt eerily recognizable, as if I already knew of the world he lived in. His world sounded too much like my own.

"Vampires live in covens, too. Each coven has four Hunters. Each Hunter is blessed with one gift: the ability to be a reader, a healer, a shielder, or a seer. It's believed that when combined, they would create an ultimate power."

"So what are you?" I asked, swallowing the knot that formed in my throat. The world of vampires was far more vast than I had every realized.

"Don't you know?" He gave me a boyish grin, and I fought to not forget what he truly was: a murderer. I couldn't let his seductive British accent or his charming looks make me forget. "Look within yourself. Find the answer."

He stood and faced me, and I took that as my cue to follow his lead. I stood before him. I focused on him with an intensity that made me shudder. I didn't know what I was doing.

And nothing happened.

Instead of tapping into some hidden vampiric power source, I just stood there, jaw clenched, digging my nails into balled fists. Needless to say, I wasn't very good at being a vampire, so I did the only thing that didn't make me look like I was constipated. I called upon spirit. I wasn't sure if I still had my Pagan powers, but the vampire seemed to think I did.

I relaxed my body, shaking away the nerves, the tightness. I closed my eyes and focused on my breath. Inhaling through my nose. Exhaling through my mouth. I pictured the world around me.

The moon had reached its peak, and as it slowly set, the sun would soon rise. I focused on her, on Mother Nature, on her power—the power that was nestled in all her children.

As a spirit user, I had a small affinity for all magic, because spirit was everywhere, in everything, but I had never perfected my skill of using the other elements for long periods of time. I reached within myself, tugging the new part of me that contained my heightened senses toward the part of me that held onto my past.

My magic encompassed me, wrapping around each crevice of my body just as it had done before I had changed. I formed a small smile.

Turning into a vampire hadn't meant losing who I was. Being a witch would always be part of me. I hadn't turned. I had transitioned—into a better, more powerful version of me. The me who made a sacrifice to become The Power's vessel. The me who made the ultimate betrayal in order to save myself and my coven.

I reached out to the vampire, placing my palm flat against his chest. His scent hit me first. His essence was cool and tingled in my lungs. He smelled of musk and mint. His heart pounded beneath my hand and in my head. I had heard it before, when the distance between us became less and less, and each time, it rang in my ears. I knew it was there, but I still hadn't expected to find a heartbeat.

One. Two. One. Two. I counted the echoing beats as if I had just regained my ability to hear. Heat pulsated from his body and radiated through me. My breathing became heavy.

As I stepped nearer, I watched as a soft glow around him shone brighter and brighter. Reaching out to it, I smiled as it swirled around my essence, wrapping me in a warm blanket of bliss. But as I pulled his magic closer to me, it began letting go, releasing my body from its grip. It left me alone. Cold. Blissless.

Sticks cracked, jolting us out of our trance. Jasik spun around, his hand easily maneuvering his blade from its sheath. He stepped before me, protectively blocking my body with his. I stepped beside him in a deviant move to show him that I didn't need his protection.

Malik stood only a few feet from us, jaw clenched, face hard. "We found something."

Jasik nodded, slid his weapon back into place, and walked away. My body ached as he left my side. The bright glow around him faded away, and I knew his magic was now out of reach.

Crossing my arms over my chest, I kicked the sticks at my feet. The lingering effects of magic took a heavy toll on my strength. After each ritual, our coven would feast. I imagined refueling a vampire was just as important.

"We mustn't speak of her to anyone," Malik said in a hushed tone. I glanced over as Jasik's face grew grim.

"Neither the time nor place," Jasik said, glancing at me. I looked away.

I ignored the vampires' obvious attempt to withhold information from me and concentrated on the ache in my gut. I was hungry, and while it irritated me that they were blatantly keeping secrets, I was too worried about what feeding actually meant.

We left the clearing and emerged into the forest, quickly picking up our pace from a brisk walk to a full-on run. While we weren't particularly near the neighboring human population, we were close enough to risk someone strolling by. These woods were known for their hiking grounds. I wondered if the vampires worried about my level of control. I shook away the concern and convinced myself that they were only worried about their own safety.

Mere minutes passed, but we ran several miles. We had run north, leaving behind California as we entered Oregon. During all of my hunts, I had never ventured this far north.

The vampires led me to a dying wolf. Its matted gray and white hair was stained with blood. As the smell hit me, a wave of hunger rocked my insides. My stomach lurched as if I hadn't eaten in days, and my tongue went dry. My muscles tightened as I rubbed my dry tongue over my lips. I began to shake, and as each second passed, it became more difficult to control the urge.

My fangs lengthened as I released a small growl. I knew I was no longer in control. The part of me that rose to the surface was more terrifying than the vampires that surrounded me. I pounced on the wolf. I gave in to the need, to everything I had prayed I'd never become.

Digging my fangs into its body, I drank hard and long. Expecting it to taste no differently than rusty water, I was surprised when the thick substance coating my tongue was refreshing. It was sweet with a hint of bitterness, but most importantly, it was delicious. My muscles felt stronger, my senses more alert. I scrunched the wolf's fur in my hands, pushing my face deeper into it; it ceased to struggle and whimper as it took its last breath.

Sticks crunched against the ground, and my head shot up. A pack of wolves emerged from behind the tree line. A large wolf stepped forward. The alpha. It released a loud growl as it continued to take steps toward me, challenging. I knew I had killed a member of its pack, and it was the alpha's duty to protect its remaining members. But I refused to give up my meal.

I jumped to my feet and sprang before it. With my foot, I pushed the carcass farther behind me. I pulled my lips up, further exposing my fangs. Streams of blood dripped down my chin, and I released a growl. The alpha met my gaze and held it, but I refused to look away. He challenged me for only seconds before they began to slowly back away. Waiting until the crunches beneath their feet were no longer audible, I relaxed my strained muscles and sat down beside the dead wolf. I finished the final slurps and licked the drips of blood from my chin.

In that moment, I had forgotten who I was. I had killed a living creature, a child of Mother Nature. As a witch, I was raised to love all living things. We hadn't abstained from eating meat, but my coven respected nature and lived peacefully among animals. We learned to give our livestock a peaceful life—and death. What I had done was a disgrace.

I stood, looking down at my hands. Chunks of gray, matted fur coated my fingers. Holding my hands up for all to see, I began to shake, and I looked at Jasik. I whimpered, my breathing coming in short bursts. I didn't know why I looked to him, but I needed someone, *anyone*, to tell me what I had just done was okay.

He took the few steps that separated us and wrapped his arms around me, digging the fingers of his free hand into my hair. He rested his chin atop my head.

"It will become easier with time. I promise."

I ignored his words. I had *killed* something. But worst of all, I had enjoyed it. I wanted him to tell me it was okay. I wanted him to make me forget. I wasn't ready to hear that it would become easier, because I never wanted it to happen again.

Pulling away from him, I wiped my hands on a patch of grass, removing all evidence of my despicable actions. I wiped my tears away with my sleeve and walked toward the others.

I was stronger than I realized, yet weaker than I wanted to admit.

Quickening my pace, I caught up to Jeremiah and Lillie, leaving Jasik and Malik behind. The two were sparring in a grassy field. They ignored me and acted as if my actions weren't uncommon. They acted as if they didn't care.

I crossed my arms over my chest and let my breathing slow. Once my fear subsided, I watched the two fight. They seemed to use only enough strength to make their next move. I watched them as a predator stalked prey. It wasn't uncommon of me: I had stalked and killed many vampires as a witch. I imagined I was fighting them. I saw openings that the other didn't notice—or didn't utilize. They fought for fun, for sport, not for victory.

"Shouldn't we be going somewhere? Someone could see, and the sun…" I asked.

"This area is rural enough, and we have some time before the sun rises. We so rarely take time off to enjoy the beauties of life. I encourage indulging in what recreational activities we can when done hunting," Jasik explained.

I said nothing. Instead, I thought about what he said. Vampires enjoying the beauties of life wasn't something I had been taught. I thought I knew everything I needed to know about the creatures I was destined to kill, but in reality, there was so much I didn't understand, so much I needed to learn.

"Lillie is our reader. Her ability to read her opponent's mind gives her an advantage, but Jeremiah's shield can prevent her from touching him. Their quarrels are quite amusing," Jasik said as he stepped beside me.

"And you're the healer," I said, remembering how his essence had merged with mine. The warmth of his healing powers seemed to still linger. I glanced up to him, noticing the soft white glow that surrounded him.

"And Malik is a seer. His ability allows him to foresee events—tragic and not." His eyes never met mine.

I returned my gaze to the fighting vampires. Just as Lillie somersaulted toward Jeremiah, an iridescent glow surrounded him, and he back-flipped away. They laughed as they fought, though both wore looks of disdain. It was clear they each didn't want to hurt the other, but neither would simply give up the fight either.

They seemed to be masters at evading each other's attacks. Being a reader, Lillie could read Jeremiah's mind, so she was able to move quicker and cheat her way out of the hit. But Jeremiah did his fair share of cheating, too. Using his ability to shield, he created blockages, forcing Lillie into corners. As each landed a hit on the other, I was sure someone would hear. Though we hid deep within the woods just north of Mt. Shasta, the force behind their blows caused an echoing vibration that radiated through the forest.

"They fight like siblings," I said with a chuckle.

"Jeremiah has only recently joined our coven."

I smiled. His newborn-ness had been apparent even when I first saw him.

"He was turned after a near fatal wound acquired during the last world war," Jasik continued. "Lillie has been with us much longer. She lost her family to the Spanish influenza. She changed willingly. Malik and I found her, dressed as a savage and living with Rogues. We almost killed her, but our realization that she could be helped saved her."

Jasik watched the two fight, his eyes growing hazy, distant, as if he were reliving those moments in history. "I couldn't imagine living forever without someone," he whispered.

His honesty made my breath catch. The only vampires I had ever encountered didn't express such emotion, such pain and longing. I knew of the pain he felt. I would remain ageless while my Pagan family would grow old and die. I'd watch as their skin turned to wrinkles. I'd watch as they took their last breaths, knowing I could offer them forever, but understanding that they would never accept my gift of eternal life, of eternal youth.

"How did you become a vampire?" I asked, curiosity getting the best of me.

"Malik and I died during the Black Plague. We lived in a small village in England. I was 25, Malik 28. We lost everything and everyone, and just as we were to take our last breaths, something came for us. We later awoke in London. We remained in hiding. Our High Priestess found us, and we have stayed with her ever since, moving from place to place, protecting our kind while simultaneously eliminating any threats."

I silently thanked the gods I had paid attention in history. Mentally doing the math, I figured Jasik had to have been born by 1320s, which made him almost 700 years old. I shook my head at the thought. I didn't understand the vampire species. How was it even possible? He didn't look a day over... 25. Why would anyone want to live that long? Sure, Jasik didn't have a choice, but Lillie had chosen this life.

I had chosen this life.

"It's time," Jasik said, breaking my silence.

"For?" I asked, confused.

"To determine your ability."

I swallowed hard, taking a step forward. If I was going to survive this new life, I needed to know what I could do. The two vampires abruptly stopped and began approaching me, as if they sensed my willingness. I was encircled by vampires, a situation I had been in before, but this time, I wasn't in it for the kill. I quivered at the thought.

I looked between them and then back to Jasik. He gave a slight nod to the others, and something hit me from the front. I was forced backward, flying through the air until I slammed against a tree. I fell to the ground, the bark scratching against my t-shirt. Dazed, I stood quickly.

The first rule of survival is to be alert. Always.

Crossing his arms, Jeremiah flashed me a wide grin. I knew he had somehow hit me with his shield. It felt like a shield of air, but more powerful. Nina's ability would have been no match.

I furrowed my eyebrows as I ran toward them. My arms swung at my sides as my feet pounded against the ground. The two stood without moving and grinned as I approached. I jumped for Lillie, leaping into the air, higher than human legs would have taken me, but she stepped to the side before I reached her. Somersaulting on the ground, I jumped back to my feet and dashed toward Jeremiah, but I skidded to a stop.

An iridescent wall shimmered before him, enclosing both him and Lillie; their bubble of protection seemed impenetrable.

"This is cheating!" I yelled, crossing my arms over my chest.

They laughed as I pouted. I wanted to learn. I needed to learn—how to fight, how to use my power, how to be a vampire. Learning everything I could to become the best, the strongest Hunter, was the quickest way to get my revenge on the Rogues who took my life from me.

"You think this is funny?" I asked, annoyed.

I took a few steps forward and placed my hand against Jeremiah's shield. Nothing happened. I balled my fist and thrust my arm back and forth. Each blow struck his shield, but the wall maintained its strength. I concentrated on the wall, on the strength to break his armor.

I thought of the strength of the earth and focused on using its energy to fuel my desire. Slowly, his wall began to give way. As it loosened, Jeremiah's face grew grim. Ignoring the two trapped inside, I focused on my arm, absorbing as much strength as I could and allowing it to flow into each hit. The wall cracked, and I drew my arm back to make my final blow, but my fist was caught mid-air.

"Stop," Jasik ordered, his hand clasping my wrist. "Look at what you're doing!"

I ripped my hand from his grip and drew my arm again, but the shield was gone. Instead, I found Jeremiah sprawled across the ground. Lillie sat down beside him.

"What happened?" I asked, lowering my arms.

"You nearly broke through his shield," Jasik said, staring at me in disbelief.

"You told me to fight!" I didn't understand his anger, his confusion.

"Avah," Jasik said, meeting my frustrated glare. "No one has ever broken Jeremiah's shield before. And many have tried."

"I… I'm sorry," I said, turning to where the vampire lay. "Jeremiah, I'm so sorry."

I sat beside him while Lillie placed his head on her lap. I was sure she didn't want me near them, but she said nothing.

"Jeremiah," I whispered as I rubbed my fingertips against his cheek. A hint of bitterness was in the air, and I inhaled deeply to welcome the scent. My fangs lowered in response as the deep red stain formed on Jeremiah's torso. Lillie, already by his side, ripped open Jeremiah's shirt, revealing a long slash embedded deep in his chest. He was badly bruised. My jaw dropped at the sight of his wounds.

Jasik fell to the ground, landing on his knees. His eyes took on an eerie glow as his fangs lowered, and he bit into his wrist. He placed his dripping wrist atop Jeremiah's chest, and blood steadily dripped into the gaping slash. Within seconds, Jeremiah's wound had healed and disappeared, and his eyes opened. Hacking, he buckled onto his side and buried his fingers in dirt. He took in quick, heavy breaths. Lillie helped lift him off the ground, keeping one of his arms around her shoulders so that he could lean on her.

I stared in disbelief, unable to stand. How could I have caused that much damage? Jeremiah was stronger than me. He had to be. How could I have gotten that close to breaking his shield? Close enough to taking his life?

Jasik offered his hand, and I took it.

"This is of no fault of yours. We did not know your strength. Jeremiah has already healed."

I ignored him. I knew Jeremiah would be okay. In all honesty, I wasn't worried about him. I was more concerned with me. I didn't understand my vampire strength, and now I was making enemies. If I was going to survive in this world, I needed to learn their rules. I had to give them a chance.

"Let's get home. Day will soon break, and Jeremiah must rest," Malik said, walking over to Jeremiah, who was now able to stand alone.

Looking at the ground, I took my walk of shame behind the vampires, hoping I'd wake up and this nightmare would be over.

"We must make haste," Jasik said, breaking my trance. "Can you keep up?"

I nodded, and we ran. My hair flew behind me as I

dashed toward the others, ignoring the growing pain in my gut. I refused to believe that I was hungry. *Already.* I ignored the trees whipping past at my sides. I focused only on the night.

The air grew heavy with mist and salt. The scent of wildflowers grew weaker. We were leaving Oregon, still heading north. The moon sat above us; its glow brightened the woods, and I was able to see night animals scurrying away. No doubt they sensed that predators were near.

I didn't know how long we ran. I just knew that I had never felt more alive or more at peace with Mother Earth. I briefly closed my eyes, listening to the creatures of the night. I inhaled deeply as the wind brushed across my cheeks. It felt like I was only at peace for mere moments, though I was sure we ran for hours. I never grew tired or wary of where the vampires were taking me. I trusted in myself and in Mother Earth. And just as I was finally coming to terms with what had happened to me, we came to a hasty stop.

A black, wrought-iron fence loomed before us. The tips pointed like deadly daggers. Two large gargoyles stood beside the wide entrance. Their menacing glares stared back at me. Witches had often used gargoyles for protection against evil entities, and I found it odd that vampires did, too.

"They're spelled," Jasik said.

I met his eyes, confused. "Witches live here?"

"No, but we've made allies," he replied.

I couldn't help gawking at him. Had he really just suggested that witches had *helped* vampires?

"There is much for you to learn," he said, his British accent thickening the words. He smiled, turned, and walked away. The other vampires had already left us behind.

I realized then that I could run. By the time they had realized I wasn't there, I could be to Montana or back home in Wisconsin. I knew I could never run back to Shasta. They'd find me there. But I could be free. Free of my Pagan expectations. Free of the vampire curse. And then I shook my head and kicked twigs at my feet.

I could *never* be free of the vampire curse, and it was time to face it: I *needed* Jasik. I wasn't very good at being a vampire.

I followed the vampires across the threshold. I had almost expected to burst into flames upon entrance, like an evil being entering holy grounds. I laughed inside at the thought. Comparing a vampire coven to holy ground? I must have lost my mind.

The overgrown grass made it difficult to navigate the stone walkway. A small cemetery sat to my right. I found myself stopping to pray for the lost souls. The headstones were stacked one after the other. I wondered how the dead fit in such close quarters.

The carvings on the front stones were dark, new. The stones in rows farther back were dirty and chipped, and the ground around them was covered in weeds. I wondered how long the oldest grave had been there. One hundred years? Five hundred? I thought back to our cemetery. Ancestry played a bigger role in the vampires' lives than I had realized.

The similarities between the two species, witches and vampires, left a bad taste in my mouth. Why, in all of my teachings, had I never learned of this side to them? Why had I never learned of Hunters, of vampires who seemed to protect me more than my own coven?

The overhanging trees were without bloom. I imagined how cold it must be. It was December, and we were in Washington. There was a light layer of snow beneath my feet. The crunch of it beneath my heels brought me home. I smiled as I remembered the long winters in Wisconsin. They seemed never-ending.

Each season brought a blizzard, and each blizzard brought games. I would play outside for hours. Only during Wisconsin winters did I learn how to control my magic, because only then did I need to call upon fire's warmth.

I lifted my arm, palm to the sky. I didn't feel cold, though I felt the breeze. I suppose I only knew it was cold because the human in me still beckoned to me. The witch wasn't letting go, after all.

I dropped my arm and slowly backed away. As I turned, I collided with Jasik, who wrapped his hands around my arms to keep me from losing my balance.

"I was just…" I said, looking over my shoulders. Only then did I see them. They glinted as the moonlight hit them just right. Runes. Runes of protection, of strength.

"We must get inside," he said, breaking my trance.

"Who's buried here?" I asked, pulling away from him. The runes spelled on the tombstones were powerful. They were meant to keep something out.

Or something in.

He said nothing.

"Jasik, *who* is buried here?" I asked again. I made a point of asking in a tone that made him understand he didn't have a choice. He *would* tell me, or we'd stay outside until the sun rose.

"Our dead," he said. His answer annoyed me. He gave me a simple, and obvious, answer—one he knew I knew was technically correct.

"Jasik," I said, breathing slowly, choosing my words wisely. "These stones are spelled. I know this, because I have used these very same spells on the graves of our dead. *Why* are these particular stones spelled, and if you lie or give me a stupid answer, I'm going to sink my fangs so deeply into your throat your healing powers wouldn't be able to fix it before the sun rose. Understand?"

He smiled. In truth, his reaction didn't surprise me as much as mine had. I had just threatened a seemingly very powerful vampire, and I wasn't worried. I knew I could take him.

I took a step forward and linked my arm with his. He tensed under my show of affection. I found it odd that my proximity always made him nervous. Vampires were used to blending in with humans, and in order to successfully blend in, you had to become comfortable. When I agreed to leave with them, I thought I would be the one having a difficult time transitioning into a new life with new rules. But in reality, we both were having a difficult time accepting the change.

"I want to trust you," I said. "You're all I know now, Jasik. As much as I hate the thought, you're all I have."

I smiled. I gave him the most sincere smile I could muster. I didn't want to fight with him. I needed him to see that he could trust me, too.

There was no space between us. My body rested against his. His heartbeat rose as I met his eyes. As much as I wanted to play the friend game, I still didn't like how comfortable I was becoming with him. I tried to tell myself that I had to remember who I was—even if I wasn't entirely sure I wanted to remain that same girl. But I knew my survival rested in his hands, and I needed to know that I could count on him when it mattered most. I needed to know that he wouldn't pounce the moment my back was turned.

"The tombstones imprison those of us turned

Rogue. They're no longer living, but we take extra precautions. Thus, the stones and graveyard are spelled."

"How do we turn Rogue?" I whispered. I barely heard my own words, even with my heightened senses, but it was all I could say.

"By giving into the blood lust, by feeding from humans to the point where you consume their essence. It triggers a change—one from which you cannot return."

I looked back over my shoulder, staring at the tombstones. I hadn't noticed the mausoleum hidden in the corner. I wondered what was in there. Most of the dead seemed to be buried in the ground. Who was important enough to be buried behind what I assumed to be a locked door?

I unlinked my arm and walked beside him in silence. Within minutes, a large, dark building emerged from the smoky air. A Victorian mansion. Its wraparound stone porch and stained-glass windows would spook even the strongest heart. More gargoyles sat beside the entrance to the porch and were perched on the roof. Figures stood in the windows of the upper floors, watching us. I swallowed hard. I knew more vampires were inside. I was just getting used to Jasik and the Hunters. How was I to live in a house full of them?

"Everything will be okay," Jasik said as he squeezed my hand.

I realized he'd promised that twice tonight, and I was beginning to wonder if he was actually trying to reassure himself.

CHAPTER
FIVE

JASIK PUSHED THE double doors open, and we filed inside.

The door closed behind us, locking us in. I folded my arms over my chest as I looked around. We were in a foyer. A grand staircase wide enough for all five of us to walk up side-by-side was before me. I glanced to my left; black leather couches sat beside massive double doors. Vampires whispered amongst each other as I scanned the room. Mirrors and artwork adorned the walls.

I turned around, finding Malik standing directly behind me, blocking my path to the door. The walls held an old mirror. I stared at the girl looking back at me. Her violet eyes looked bright and full of life. Yet, I felt empty inside—and alone in a house full of vampires. I cringed and held my arms tighter around my body.

The floors were a dark wood while the walls were painted light beige. A Gothic chandelier hung above me, allowing dim lighting, but my eyes adjusted to the darkness. Many of the lingering vampires welcomed the Hunters home with various greetings: pats on the backs, hugs, kissing cheeks. I received nothing but stares and whispered gossip, as if my vampire ears couldn't pick up the disgust in their tones. I wondered if they knew what I was: part witch, part vampire.

The room directly to our right was a large conservatory. Large gray and black stained-glass bay windows allowed in moonlight, and I couldn't help but wonder how the vampires survived the mornings in a room with floor-to-ceiling windows.

The Hunters led me up the stairs, allowing me extra peeks into the conservatory's adjoining room: a library closed off by glass French doors. I had been an English minor while in college, so I was easily able to imagine myself spending hours each day in there. I was sure it would be my only peace while in the house.

When we reached the top, Jasik took several steps forward and opened the door directly in front of us, and the vampires piled in. Lillie pushed past me, slamming into my shoulder, and took a place beside the woman sitting behind a large, dark-wooded desk.

The woman's hands were folded atop the table before her. She stared at me, her eyes moving up and down my body. I dropped my arms, allowing them to dangle by my sides, and squeezed my hands. Between her dark, mocha-colored skin; long, black locks; and bright green eyes, she was absolutely beautiful. Breaking the gaze that felt a lot like a game of mercy, I glanced around the room.

Behind the woman, a large window brought in lines of moonlight, and in the distance, I watched waves crash into the large rocks surrounding the back of the manor. I hadn't realized we were so close to the ocean. I didn't understand how I could possibly have missed the scent of salt water.

Both walls to my right and left were covered with floor-to-ceiling bookshelves. Dust coated the shelves and tickled my nose. Each book fit tightly into its place, leaving no room for extras. I imagined one led to a secret room just like I'd seen on a television show as a child. I assessed each shelf, looking for a hint of cleanliness or fingerprints to betray their secret passageway.

The woman cleared her throat and said, "Jasik, I hope to hear all went well with our problem." She spoke loudly, affirmatively, eliminating any doubt that she wasn't the head of this house.

"Yes, Milady," he said. "We were able to eliminate most of the Rogues. Very few survived." He stood tall, one arm resting behind his back and the other at his side. I noticed that the other Hunters mimicked this same stance, and I wondered if I should match them. I released the grip in my hands and stood straighter. I began pulling my arm behind my back, but a glance from Malik stopped me dead in my track.

"And who is this?" she asked, looking me over once again, stopping at my eyes. I couldn't decide if that was because people typically look one another in the eyes or if it was because mine were so obviously different from those around me.

"We encountered another problem. A coven of witches was attacked, and I was forced to change her." Thu-thump. Thu-thump. Thu-thump-thump. Thu-thump-thump. I listened as Jasik's heartbeat rose when he finished his sentence. He clenched his fist behind his back, and his heart rate slowed again. His hesitation was minimal and probably unnoticed by the beauty before us, but any hesitation led me to believe I might have to fight my way out of this death chamber.

Lillie met my gaze, her jaw clenching. I didn't understand why she disliked me. I knew it wasn't only Jeremiah's close call that brought on such hatred.

The woman cleared her throat and stood, placing just her fingertips against the desk. "You know the law, Jasik."

"I do, and I am prepared to repent for my actions."

My breath caught in my throat. Repent? As in die? If they were willing to kill *him,* what the hell would they do to *me?*

"I see she is a Hunter. What is her ability?" she asked.

"We're unsure."

"Uncover her ability tomorrow, and I will find placement for her in another coven. You may leave."

"Another coven?" I blurted. "I don't want to go to another coven." I turned to Jasik. The thought of meeting even more vampires who hated me made my blood boil. And I was getting really tired of making new friends.

His jaw clenched. I immediately regretted my outburst. I was sure I had broken some super-secret vampire law.

"Milady," he began, "she will need to be trained in both combat and the way of our people. I will gladly complete this task, but it may be beneficial to the coven if she is placed here."

"We do not need another Hunter," she said, stepping away from behind her desk.

"Having another on location could prove ideal. Had Rogues attacked in our absence…" He didn't finish. I supposed he didn't need to.

I waited what seemed like an eternity for her decision. "I'll consider it. You may leave." And in the end, I still didn't get one.

The door closed behind us after we left the room. I turned on my heel and faced the stairway, unsure of where to go. Another closed door was to my left, and a long hallway stretched down my right. Hoping we didn't have to go back downstairs, I looked up to Jasik, noticing that he was already watching me.

"This way," he said, walking down the hallway. Relief

washed over me. I was able to avoid the vampires downstairs... for now.

As we walked side by side, I looked back to Jeremiah, who was swarmed by a dozen or so girls. His swoon ability was in full effect. I smiled when he looked over to me, and to my surprise, he smiled back.

We walked past a lounge, which sat nestled in a corner beside the office we had just left. We continued down the hall and past several sets of doors.

"I'll see you tomorrow," Malik said. Jasik nodded, and I looked back to meet Malik's goodbye. He turned away and disappeared through the first closed door to our left.

"No one wants me here," I said. I wasn't sure why it bothered me. I *really* didn't want to be here anyway, right? I didn't belong here. The pit in my stomach grew deeper as I realized I didn't belong anywhere.

"You're with me. You're welcomed wherever I am," Jasik replied.

You're with me. My heart dropped as he said those words. But why? His arm brushed against mine as we walked down the hall, and heat surged through my body. My heart began to race at his proximity. The lingering smell of his musk teased my senses. I shook my head. I needed sleep. I needed to learn to control my senses.

The hallway we walked down was long and dark. The same dark-wooded floors were beneath my heels, and another Gothic-looking chandelier lit our way. I expected to find sconces, stone floors, and blood-stained walls, but instead, though dark, it felt like a home. Like it could be *my* home. I tried to clear my thoughts.

"We passed Malik's room," he said. "Mine's here, and this will be yours." His room sat between mine and Malik's.

"Jeremiah and Lillie?" I asked.

He turned and faced the doors across from ours. The door across from mine was for guests, the room across from Jasik's was Lillie's, and the room across from Malik's was Jeremiah's. He went on to explain that the other members of the coven resided on the third and fourth floors.

"I'll show you the rest of the manor tomorrow, but we needn't go up there."

I turned back to my door and walked in. The bedroom was stunning. A king-sized bed dressed in dark maroon sat directly in front of me, supported by four posts that nearly touched the ceiling. Sheer white fabric twirled around each post and then enclosed the bed, creating a blissful paradise. An enormous armoire sat to the right, made of the same dark-brown wood as the rest of the manor. An elegant make-up table angled in the corner to my left. The enormity of the furniture made the room feel small, yet comforting.

"The door to your left is your personal bathroom, and the one to your right is your closet," Jasik said, breaking my awestruck moment.

"Thank you," I said, turning back to him. "For everything." It was clear that Jasik had risked his life for me. I still didn't understand why, and I wondered if I would have done the same for him.

He smiled, nodded, and then stepped backward, grabbing onto the door handle.

"We must rise early, by eight in the evening. Sleep well, Avah."

"Night," I said with a small smile.

He turned to leave. Before the door latched, he added, "Stay in your room tonight."

And with that, the door closed, leaving me alone with my racing thoughts and mixed feelings.

Leaning against the closed door, I looked around the room. I flipped the lights off, peeled off my clothes, and slipped into the nightgown that was conveniently left on the bed. Settling in under the covers, I hoped for sleep.

But rather than its welcoming embrace, I projected.

I sat up, looking around. My head felt heavy, the room dark. As I stood and rose from the bed, it took all of my effort to take just a few steps. I looked around the room, noticing the corner, full-length mirror, the cracked wall, the shattered pictures. I leaned down and picked one up.

The collage was of a beautiful girl. She smiled next to an older woman who closely resembled her. They hugged each other as if nothing could tear apart their bond. In the next, she stood with an arched back, strong legs, and straight arms pointed toward the sky. I looked past the girl wearing a metallic, sparkly leotard; others matched her stance, but they stood on beams, preparing to twirl and jump and maintain balance. In the final picture, the girl was kissing a boy. His brown hair was shaven short, and her hand was wrapped around his neck, pulling him closer to her.

The girl looked happy, as if life had given her

everything she had asked for: family, friends, romance. Faces were the ultimate disguise for the turmoil that lay beneath. The girl in the picture was used to hiding her inner desires, and the boy in the picture had no idea. But then again, she had everyone fooled.

I set the picture on the bedside table and walked around the bed, trailing my hand against the footboard. The door across from the end of the bed was open, and clothes cluttered the floor. She must have left so abruptly that she didn't have time to clean. Maybe when she returned. I closed the door, hiding the mess from unwelcome eyes.

A scattering of post-it notes decorated the front of the door.

Write more poetry.

Help Mrs. Mills with garden.

Clean closet.

Russian History test on Monday.

A floorboard creaked. I turned around, but no one was there.

The air became hazy as I walked to the desk that sat beside the closet. Homemade picture frames with super-glued seashells stuck to the corners. The happy girl sat at a table surrounded by smiling faces. She, too, smiled, wrapping her arms around shoulders and waists. A closed laptop, an open notebook with scribbled cartoons, and a stack of books: English Literature 1800s, Russian History, Astrology, and Economics. Against the desk, a backpack sat open on the floor. Folders, notebooks, and pens spilled out.

I grabbed a lanyard off the desk; *Northern Shasta College - California* was written across the strap. I stared at the girl in the picture on the ID. Her long brown hair rested in soft waves next to her face. Her smile seemed to stretch from ear to ear. *Senior* was written below the headshot and *Home of the Bears* below that.

"She looks so happy," I said.

"You were," a voice said from behind me.

I dropped the lanyard and spun around, taking a step back.

"Are you still happy, Avah? Are they… taking care of you?"

The woman standing before me was the same woman in the broken frame that now lay on the bedside table. The woman holding the happy girl.

I shook my head and took a few more steps back,

tears threatening.

"Avah, you have to accept who you are. You can't fight fate. This happened for a reason. Please don't forget that. You were chosen for a reason," she said with a smile.

My eyes burned. "No," I said, shaking my head.

"It's okay. You don't have to hide anymore," she said as she took a few steps toward me. She reached her arms out, waiting for me to fall into the hug.

Tears streamed down my cheeks, and I finally gave in. I leapt toward her. We fell to the ground sobbing. She caressed my head, brushing hair from my eyes. "I'm so scared," I said. "I'm so alone."

"You're never alone. I will always be with you," she said as she planted a kiss atop my head.

I nodded, and she wiped away the tears.

"Now, stop crying. We don't have a lot of time. Listen to me. Believe in yourself. Fight your hardest, and don't let them change you. Your heart is so full of love. You're strong. You can make it through this. I miss you, Avah, and I'll love you forever."

CHAPTER
SIX

I WOKE TO the blaring alarm on my bedside table. Reaching over, I slammed my hand down on the top button, silencing the abrasive beeps.

7:15 pm.

I rolled back over and stared at the ceiling. With thick shades hanging over the windows, darkness engulfed my room, yet I could see everything, as if the sun was setting, casting shadows in corners while illuminating patches of floorboards. I ran my fingers through my matted hair and took a deep breath. I yanked the covers off and walked into the bathroom.

Staring at a set of violet irises, I leaned against the countertop. Stopping just inches away from the mirror, I curled my lips and ran my tongue over my teeth, emphasizing the pointy tips of my canines. They were retracted, but they hung ever so slightly lower than a human's, giving away their hopeless attempt at normality.

Fangs: meant for ripping through flesh, tearing away everything that being once was. Fangs meant death. No, fangs meant murder. Vampires needed blood to survive. *I* needed blood to survive. Whether that meant killing a human or an animal, it left an acidic sting in my gut.

Murder. No matter what word you chose to describe it, it was wrong. Like I should know better. Immoral. Could vampires have morals? Witches fought for morals, for life. Vampires fought for blood... for life. The sickening twist of what life meant for two different beings left a bad taste in my mouth. I pulled away from the mirror and shook my head. I swallowed hard, grabbing a tube of toothpaste.

After brushing, I jumped into the shower, letting the water rush down my body, swirling into the drain at my feet. I curled my toes and then shot them forward, flinging water as they returned to their rightful place. After what felt like hours, I stepped out of the glass enclosure. Wrapping myself in the towel, I padded across the bedroom floor, leaving a trail of wet footprints in my wake.

I opened the door to the closet and gawked at its enormity. To my left sat an array of clothes. From tops to bottoms to evening wear, each section was color-coordinated and sorted neatly together. To my right sat all the shoes money could buy. At least, that's what I assumed. Boots, heels, and sneakers, they sat in special, perfectly-sized cubbies. I ran my fingers against the clothes that hung on hooks. Shelves were stacked against the far wall directly across from the door.

I walked toward the shelves, dropping my towel as I grabbed a black sports bra with a crisscrossed back. I slipped on the bra and grabbed the matching pair of boy-shorts. Sliding them on, I yanked a pair of calf-length leggings off a hook. I pulled on the closest shirt and stepped into a pair of ballet flats, kicking the door closed with my foot as I left.

I twisted my long hair into a French braid that wrapped around my shoulder and hung down the side of my chest. With one last look in the mirror, I closed the door to my room behind me.

My mother was right: I had to give this new life everything I had, even if being this *thing* was more than I could bear. Embracing my new destiny as a Hunter would enable me to kill the Rogues who stole everything from me. I was stronger and faster now. Once I learned to control my power, nothing could stop me. I smiled at the thought, sucking in a deep breath and walking the few steps down the hall to Jasik's room.

"Come in," a voice said before my hand had touched the wood of Jasik's door.

I turned the handle and stepped inside, closing the door behind me.

His room was almost identical to mine. Rather than maroon, his was navy blue, and where my make-up table sat, his room contained a desk. Stacks of books were piled on the floor next to an overflowing bookshelf. Their musty smell filled the room with a familiar, home-like aroma. Pictures of cities and landscapes were staggered on the walls—each beautiful in its own way. A city skyline, a country cabin, mountains, and oceans, their diverse images had one common theme: a sunrise.

Jasik stood next to his bed, shirtless. His hair was damp, and water droplets trickled down his forehead. Thick layers of muscle covered his torso. My heart thumped faster as I admired his body, just as I had his room. His chest rose and fell quickly, matching my breath. His arms rested by his sides, his hands clenched with white knuckles. My vision became blurred; the space between us, though distant, felt somehow intimate.

"I'll just—I'll wait outside," I said, turning away and grabbing onto the door handle.

He said nothing as I slipped out the door and slammed it behind me. Leaning against the wall, I tipped my head back and closed my eyes, waiting for my sputtering heart to slow. What was wrong with me? I hated what I was, what *he* was. But I couldn't deny the attraction. After several deep breaths, I opened my eyes to find Jasik beside me, his eyes hard, concerned.

"Time for that tour?" I said, hoping we'd never have to mention what had just happened. My arm brushed his as I walked past. The tiny hairs rose, and a tingle shot through my body. I told myself it was just physical attraction. My body didn't understand what he was. I hoped the attraction would fade in time.

He nodded his head toward me and let his eyes trail down my body. As his gaze lingered, I felt oddly vulnerable. As if it were purely instinct, I stood straighter and pulled my stomach in, noticing how the leggings and short-sleeved t-shirt tightly covered my skin, as if they were merely an extension of it. In my human life, I had been a gymnast. My small frame was thin, muscular, but under his blue-eyed gaze, I felt as though *I* would never be good enough, as if I couldn't compare to his perfection.

I glanced over and took in his attire. He wore black athletic shorts that cut off just below the knees and a dark gray, sleeveless t-shirt. My eyes lingered on his muscular arms before shamefully looking away.

"The manor has four floors, an attic, and a basement. The coven's bedchambers reside on the top two floors. The attic is for storage. We will spend most of our time today in the basement, where we store weapons and have rooms designed for training."

His final words caused my eyebrow to rise, but I remained silent as we walked down the hall.

"This is the Hunters' wing. We'll begin with the main level."

"Wouldn't it make more sense to separate the Hunters? I mean, it's our job to protect the manor from Rogues, right?"

"Yes, from Rogues and other things."

"Other things? Like what?" Deep down, I knew what he meant, but I wouldn't admit it. I *couldn't* admit it. This new life had too many rules, too many changes.

He exhaled loudly and brushed a hand through his hair. He wouldn't meet my eyes.

"What things?" I asked again, daring him to answer.

"Your first lesson: you are a Hunter, Avah. It is a Hunter's job to protect his or her coven from any threat. We remain united, since our strength lies in our gifts. Our abilities connect us. Separating would make us vulnerable, and if the Hunters fall, the coven will soon follow."

His words stopped me abruptly, and I couldn't help what I blurted next. "Have you killed witches here before?" I knew it was a stupid question. Of course he had. It's what vampires do, but I needed to hear him say it. I needed to know. I needed a reason to hate him.

He stood before me, furrowing his brows and frowning. Years seemed to pass before he spoke. The conflict on his face betrayed his need to choose his words wisely, so I braced myself for the moment—the moment I'd hate him forever. Hating him granted me freedom from this place, because leaving seemed as simple as walking out the front door. Or so I thought.

"As you well know, I, too, have done what I've needed to do." He began walking away as if that alone would answer my questions.

Unsatisfied, I said, "What does that even mean?" I brought my arms up in question. When he didn't stop, I reached for him, but he slipped from my grip. "Jasik!" I yelled as my fangs dropped and a force erupted within me—powerful and pissed off. It rippled through my body, pushing out in waves through my core. An iridescent glow slammed into his back, thrusting him into the air before he tumbled to a stop.

Dazed, he looked up at me from the ground, gripping the back of his head. Standing, he brought his blood-coated hand before him and wiped it on his black shorts, removing any evidence.

I brought my hands before me in a silent plea and stared at my palms. I looked for traces of difference. My hands, my arms, my stomach, they looked the same, yet foreign. Nothing had changed physically. The force was powerful, like nothing I had ever felt.

I met his gaze, scared and confused. I fell into him, letting his strong embrace maintain my weight.

"What's wrong with me?" I asked.

"Avah," he said, pushing away strands of hair from my face. "There's nothing wrong with you."

"I can't control it. This power. I don't know what it is; I don't understand it," I said as tears dripped down my face. All I wanted was to go home. To run to my mom, to the elders, to my friends, and beg for forgiveness and to be taken back. This new world was awful and confusing and too hard.

Ever so lightly, he wiped the tears from my cheeks with his thumb.

"I promise you will learn control."

"How can you be so sure?" I said between hiccups.

"I will teach you." His words were soothing. They continued to have that effect on me. I didn't like his control over my emotions, but at that moment, I was thankful. Though, I was sure I couldn't survive without him. "You tapped into your ability. That was your shield." He smiled.

I dropped my arms and placed my fingers across my teeth. My thumbs rubbed against the fangs. Tapping into my vampire powers forced my fangs to retract. They lowered as my emotions rose—their own fight or flight response.

"Take a few deep breaths. It'll pass."

A door slammed shut behind us, and I whirled around, growling at the idea of an intruder. I was too vulnerable. I needed to learn control and master my senses.

"Calm down," Lillie said. "And put your game face away. You wouldn't stand a chance." She pushed her shoulder into mine as she passed. I imagined a vampire coven would be similar to wolves. In a pack, I was the weakest. I needed to earn my place. Simply being sired by Jasik wasn't enough.

"Lillie," Jasik said. "Enough." If I had any doubt that he wasn't the alpha in this Hunter pack, then his stance now eliminated my concern. His tone was hard, demanding. His look was challenging. Lillie shrugged off my worry and walked away.

Jasik turned back to me and held out his hand. "Come on," he said softly. "You need to feed."

I grabbed his hand and stood. Taking his advice, I swallowed hard, closed my eyes, and forced myself to relax. As I released each breath, I felt a calmness wash over me. I brushed my tongue across the edges of my teeth and was relieved to feel normal again. I opened my eyes.

"Better?" he asked with a smile.

"Better," I said. "Is this going to be the most awkward breakfast I've ever had?"

"In time, they'll learn to accept you just as you will learn to accept them."

We reached the lounge and began walking down the stairs and into the foyer. I remained silent, taking in my surroundings again. There were only a few lingering vampires, but mostly, the room was empty.

"After breakfast, we'll spend the day training. To stay, you must prove your worth," he said, without meeting my eyes.

"My *worth*? What does that even mean?" I said as we reached the bottom step.

"Vampires are always welcomed to join a coven, but Hunters must fight for their place. Your duty will be to protect the coven. You will need to know how to use your gift, how to fight, how to think, how to kill."

Jasik opened the two large double doors to our right. "This is the grand hall. We often hold parties, council meetings, events. New Year's Eve masquerade ball is next Thursday."

"A ball? People still have balls?" I said, stepping into the room.

"Yes, often."

I wondered if he would ever relax. His answers were always serious; his voice was always concerned. He seemed to fear for me more than I feared for myself. That realization made me question everything I thought I knew about vampires. At the moment, hiding behind a masquerade mask seemed highly appealing.

The dark wood flooring continued into the room, as did the light beige walls. Floor-to-ceiling windows made up the wall to my left. I had decided massive windows were a house favorite since nearly every room had them. The wall across from our entrance had two sets of French doors, and another small door sat nestled in a corner to our right. Aside from that, the room was empty. No tables. No pictures. Just windows, paint, and doors. The room was long and wide. I didn't doubt that over a hundred bodies could sit comfortably in there.

"Those doors lead to the garden," he said, nodding at the French doors across from us. "And that door," he said, pointing to the tiny door in the corner, "leads to the kitchen. And if we go back into the foyer, I'll show you the conservatory." His voice echoed through the room as he spoke. If he wasn't a vampire, he would make a great tour guide.

My eyes lingered on the doorway that led to the kitchen. What was I expected to eat now?

I turned to face him. "I will *not* kill someone, Jasik. You need to know that." It was abrupt, and I was sure I said that more for myself than him.

"We don't kill people, Avah. We're not fiends. We feed from three sources: animals, blood bags, and the willing."

I cringed at the thought of being fed from.

"'The willing?' Why are they so willing anyway? Are you offering immortality as a perk to being an on-call meals-on-wheels or something?" I said, looking around.

"Absolutely not. Turning you was unacceptable, and I will take the sentencing Amicia hands down."

"Yeah, about that. What exactly is going to happen?" I was slightly concerned that my *savior* was going to die soon, and then I'd be left with Malik, Jeremiah, or worse, Lillie. I shuddered.

"We have laws in place that make it so only High

Priestesses can change humans. It's for both power and population control. If vampires ruled the world, we'd all die. We need humans to survive."

"Then why would anyone ask to be fed from?"

He stopped and turned to me, giving a grin that made my heart stop. Only then did I notice the dimples that formed when he smiled, the strong line of his jaw, and the five o'clock shadow that aged him perfectly. "Because it's *highly* erotic."

My breath caught in my throat as his eyes burned into mine, their glow growing brighter as speckles of black tainted their color. He wet his lips. Moments seemed to drag on forever before he finally took the few steps toward me. I backed into the wall, not sure I was ready for him. He stopped when he reached me, leaving only one step between us. His breathing was slow, heavy, matching mine. His eyes invited me to him, and as much as his eyes begged me to accept his invitation, I didn't know if I could. I loved that he let me be the one to choose whether or not we broke the barrier and took that final step.

I could lose myself in him; I knew this. And what I feared more than vampires, more than my coven finding out about this forbidden romance, more than fighting a thousand Rogues at once, was that my insatiable appetite for ending this war was so easily subdued by my growing attraction to the vampire who stood before me. My body felt ready. My heart felt ready. But my mind told me it was wrong. I needed to remember that once I defeated the Rogues who did this to me, to my coven, I would return to them. I had to believe that they'd welcome me back with open arms; they'd congratulate me on controlling what I had become and using my newfound power to protect the witches. Losing myself in Jasik wasn't my fear. Losing what I could reobtain with my coven was what terrified me.

His thumb rubbed against the angle of my jaw, sending shivers through my body. "Avah," he said in his thick British accent. His voice, his plea, betrayed his longing for me, for love.

"Jasik?" a voice said, forcing us back to reality. The blackness in his eyes quickly vanished, and he dropped his arm, stepping back and clearing his throat.

Lillie stood before us. I pushed myself off the wall and crossed my arms. What had I just done? My fangs ached. I was so close to feeding from him—close enough to want to.

"Lillie," I said, my heart still pounding in my chest, my senses still erotically high. "He was just, um, giving me a tour. We didn't hear you come in."

"I'm not sure how you could," she said, annoyed and turning on her heel. "You know, most pay with their lives for the betrayal you two have committed," she added before disappearing through the door.

Her words stung. Why had I taken it so far with him? I wondered if her hatred stemmed from more than me being a witch. I wondered if she and Jasik had once been more than friends. I shook my head and looked at the ground, hoping the awkward moment would quickly pass.

I could feel Jasik's eyes on me, but I couldn't look at him. I walked away, leaving the room and Jasik behind. I didn't know what to say. I didn't know what to do. I didn't know how to fix this, these feelings that grew stronger and stronger as each minute passed. I knew I needed to make them go away, but I didn't know if I wanted to.

Jasik felt good, real. In a world where I questioned everything I was, everything I knew, I didn't question him—or his feelings for me. The way he looked at me, the way he said my name, the way he made the others keep their distance, I knew there was something there. A simple attraction that could grow into an epic love that lasted until the end of time. I was foolish to believe in such fairytales.

I had only been a vampire for a day, and I already had to remind myself that the emotions I was feeling were for a *vampire*.

I cleared my mind by focusing on the tour. I needed to learn my way around the house. I had an ache in my gut that told me Jasik wouldn't always be there to watch over me.

Jasik joined me in the foyer and, thankfully, respected my wish to not discuss what had happened. Instead, he explained that there were three rooms directly across from the grand hall: first, the conservatory. Its openness had made this room easily viewable when I had first arrived. It had no doors. Instead, two beams offered a grand entrance. There were more wall-to-wall, gray and black stained-glass windows. A fireplace was nestled in the corner, and groups of over-sized chairs gave the room a comfortable vibe. I focused on the room and its decor—anything to stop Jasik's presence from reminding me that no matter how much I tried, I didn't, I couldn't, hate him. Instead, I wanted him. I wanted him so badly it left a pit in my gut.

"You know, conservatories are for growing plants and such, but since sunlight isn't a vampire's friend…" I hoped he'd take the cue and explain why they'd have such a room in a house full of vampires. I'd talk about anything to get me to stop thinking about his proximity. My arm hairs stood on end as he stepped beside me, admiring the windows.

"Since we perish only in direct sunlight, we put in stained glass." He turned around and led me to another set of French glass doors. Pulling them open, he said, "You can get to the library from the foyer or from in here."

He closed the doors behind us.

I inhaled deeply, and the smell of musty paper filled my nostrils. It tickled my nose but soothed my nerves. The walls that did not have doors or windows held floor-to-ceiling bookshelves. More over-sized chairs sat in corners, and large tables decorated the middle of the room.

"Wow," I said, looking at the books. "There's… what? Thousands of books in here?"

"Close to, I'm sure," Jasik said.

The smell of books was overwhelming and clouded my senses. They smelled of age, of strength and dedication, and of home. I smiled at the thought. We also had a library on our property. Our elders would teach young witches the ways of our people and the threat of the vampire race. I remembered sitting on the floor with my legs crisscrossed. I would eagerly listen to the tales that had been passed down from generation to generation. We'd spend a couple hours each night in the library, listening to stories, researching vampires, learning our history.

The older I became, the more my mother pushed me to learn everything I could so that I could one day become an elder to our coven. But eventually, I grew tired of stories and games. I ventured out to experience my own life. I went to college and grew close to my classmates, but in time, I came home and devoted my life to protecting my coven.

The books sat neatly on the shelves, squeezed into the spots that seemed too small for their bindings. I jimmied a book free. Its fabric cover was peeling, as was the threaded binding. As I flipped through the pages, I saw that many were stained yellow—some no longer attached at the spine. I closed the book and ran my fingers against the divots of the title. I carefully placed it back on the shelf, gently securing it in its fragile state next to the others. It was safe between the other books, protected. I looked down at my hand and then back to the book. Its torn cover gave away its hiding spot. It would never truly be safe.

I swallowed hard and turned to face Jasik.

"In training, will you teach me how to use my gift to fight?"

"Soon, but not yet." He replied without hesitation.

"Why?" I was taken aback. He spoke so surely.

"There are other things, more important things, that must be learned," he answered matter-of-factly.

I watched him as he held his stance. Without cowering under my glare, he stared back. What could possibly be more important than learning to fight the Rogues who did this to me?

"Like what?"

"I will not teach you to fight until you are ready to

survive."

"What's the difference?" I had fought, and killed, vampires. I knew how to survive. His attitude annoyed me, and I wondered if I could best him right now.

He sighed. "My point exactly."

I folded my arms and shifted my weight from foot to foot. I wouldn't let up. I wouldn't let this go until he gave me an answer. He dropped his folded arms and leaned against the desk.

"You must first learn that there are herbs that can quicken your healing process. You must learn that at this altitude, you can run for half a day before you must feed. You must learn exactly where to stake a vampire to result in immediate death. You need to learn that taking another's life is the most important thing you'll ever do, and you need to learn that fighting isn't the only knowledge that leads to survival. Until you're ready to kill whatever stands before you—a child, an elder, a *witch*— it's not worth the time it will take to train you in combat."

He stood abruptly and walked to a new set of French doors—the ones that would lead us back into the foyer. He opened the door and stepped through, but I didn't follow. I stood, arms crossed, jaw tight. His words echoed through my mind.

Until you're ready to kill whatever stands before you...

Could I do it? Could I kill someone? Could I kill a witch? If my life depended on it, would that make it easier? Could I do it to protect myself? To protect someone I loved?

I met Jasik's eyes. He remained in the foyer, holding the door open, seemingly awaiting my decision.

"I will prove that I'm *worth* your time," I said as I walked past him. I hoped my words hurt as they left my lips. I hoped they hit his ears with a dagger-like vengeance. When I turned around to face him, he still stared at the empty library.

He closed the door after a few more seconds and walked to the end of the foyer. To our right was another lounge, and directly in front of us was a large room with opened double doors. Several long tables that fit at least a few dozen were all that the room contained. The dining hall, I was sure of it.

I took a step forward and stopped in the doorway. The tables were packed with vampires. There were so many that I was sure the entire coven was in this room.

They slurped on their straws, finishing their breakfasts. I put on a brave face and hoped it would suffice.

My mind flashed back to Amicia's threat of tossing me out, but she said she'd wait until Jasik taught me the way of her people, until I could prove my worth. I didn't see her now, but I was sure she was watching me—watching and waiting. This was a test; it had to be. She wanted to see how I'd react when I was surrounded by the creatures I had promised to kill.

Jasik lowered his hand to the middle of my back and slightly nudged me forward. We walked into the room together.

The vampires fell silent as I entered, but I ignored their devious grins and glares. Instead, I focused on the blood. Though I fought it, it was instinct. I inhaled deeply; the smell was intoxicating.

A rookie mistake.

I squeezed my hands shut until my knuckles went white. The thick aroma in the air was overpowering, tickling, poking, and prodding at my desire to feed. I couldn't break down, not in front of the entire coven, not when everyone was sure I would fail. Though the thought made my stomach turn, I couldn't be condemned from *two* covens in less than 24 hours.

That would be pathetic.

My heart pounded in my chest, and I fought to control my desire. My breathing became heavy; my fangs lengthened. I swallowed hard, but suddenly, my throat was dry. I bit my lower lip. I was losing my grasp on reality. I was a lioness stalking her prey, and just as I was about to pounce, Jasik grabbed my hand, intertwining his fingers with mine.

I barely heard the others gasp around us—at his public indiscretion. I was grateful for his devotion since it was clear that the others wanted to make a meal of me.

"You're strong, Avah. Stronger than you know. Control it," he whispered, squeezing my hand in his, grounding me. His voice was smooth; his words coated my mind in a protective layer even as my grasp on reality was threatening to break.

Bile crept its way into my mouth, my stomach lurching from hunger. I dug my nails into his hand, breaking his skin. And suddenly, the world went silent. The gasping vampires and their whispers and sputtering hearts went mute as I focused on the blood dripping down Jasik's hand.

I turned to face him, fangs pressing against my bottom lip, begging for their release. His wounds healed almost as quickly as they opened; I pulled him close to me, and he welcomed it. I released his hand and wrapped an arm behind his neck, pulling us tightly together.

In a display that brought sound back to the world I had just silenced, he tilted his head ever so slightly to the side: a show of submissiveness. My eyes widened at the vein throbbing beneath his skin, and I growled at the gasps that broke my concentration.

"Avah," he whispered. His voice was enough to tame the tide exploding within me.

I squeezed my eyes shut, focusing on taking deep, long breaths. I was shaking, but I ignored it and everything that distracted me from my control. I knew if I gave in now, I would never get myself out of the hole I'd dug. When I finally opened my eyes, Jasik stood before me, arms crossed, eyes in a knowing slant, and mouth curved into a satisfied line. I didn't know when I'd released him from my grasp. "I knew you could do it," he said. "With time, you'll learn to completely control your blood lust."

I swallowed hard and turned to face the crowd.

Slowly, the vampires surrounding me returned to their conversations, slurping away on crimson-stained straws.

Jasik and I found a table nestled in the far corner of the room. Almost immediately after we sat down, another vampire approached our table and stood beside me with a disapproving glare. I stared back; I refused to quiver under the pressure.

The vampire nodded in Jasik's direction before setting down two glasses and walking away.

"Drink." He lifted his glass in a cheering manner and chugged the liquid. After only a few gulps, it was gone. Jasik's neon irises glowed with hunger, and his fangs lengthened slightly. He ran his tongue over his lips, licking stray droplets that beaded in the corners of his mouth.

I clasped my hand around the cup and held it up, eye level. The fluid was thick and smeared the side of the glass as I swooshed it around. I closed my eyes and brought it to my lips.

The heavy liquid coated my mouth and dripped down my throat. I pulled the glass away—still half full— and ran my tongue into the crevices of my mouth. The sweet substance brought clarity with it—one I wasn't ready for.

The pulsing of the steady heartbeats around me pounded in my head. The moonlight filtering through the stained-glass windows burned against my eyes. The sweet scent of the vampires' allure clouded my nose. The cup beneath my palm tickled my fingertips, sending chills down my spine.

But the blood—the blood coursing through veins, splashing in cups, dripping down chins—the blood was everywhere. And I wanted it. I *needed* it.

Jasik twirled his fingers in the air, and another round of blood was placed on our table. I threw my head back and downed the rest of my drink. I licked my lips as I grabbed the next cup, finishing it almost as soon as the cup left the tabletop. Still unsatisfied, I reached for Jasik's cup.

"Slow down, Avah. There's plenty. Remember, you're learning control," he said, resting his hand on my outstretched arm.

I growled as he nudged my arm back. Before I realized the severity of my need, before I could stop myself, I bared fangs.

The energy in the room shifted—slight breezes brushed against my skin. The noise once again ceased, and with a speed I never knew I had, I leapt from my seat and pushed myself against the wall of windows. Most of the room had cleared, but the remaining vampires, the ones who witnessed my daring challenge against their protector, stood before me—fangs exposed, bodies tense, irises black with anger.

"Stop!" Jasik said as he stood and stepped protectively in front of me. "Go. Now."

The others relaxed, leaving the room but never letting their eyes stray from where I stood until walls separated us. I knew Jasik held a position of power in his coven, but I hadn't realized so many would so readily obey his orders.

He turned to face me, stepping nearer until there were only a few inches between us.

"Are you okay?" he asked, brushing his thumb against my bare arm. My skin tingled beneath his touch.

I didn't answer.

"Come. Training will help you focus."

I nodded and followed him out of the dining hall, leaving my final cup of blood behind.

CHAPTER
SEVEN

THE BASEMENT TRAINING quarters weren't what I was expecting. Even though the basement beautifully matched the manor's Gothic theme, I had still expected the basement out of a horror film: gloomy, cement floors, goo-covered walls, broken windows, dead bodies sprawled about.

Wall sconces provided minimal lighting in the tight and winding hallway, but my eyes adjusted quickly. It took only seconds for the shadows to dissipate. We passed a few doors as we approached the end of the hallway.

"What's down here?" I asked.

"The armory, our training room, storage, and such." I raised an eyebrow at the *armory* part. "Believe it or not," he continued, "we don't simply awaken with the skills needed to kill."

"Of course not. That would be too easy."

The training room was behind the second to last door. The room was massive. I did quick calculations in my head; there was no way this all fit under the manor. The wall to the left was floor-to-ceiling mirrors, and I wondered if the CIA would be recording my first training session. I awkwardly tugged at my clothes, not liking the feeling of someone watching without me knowing. It was clear that paranoia was setting in, but I didn't care. I turned my back to the eavesdroppers, hoping I could stay at this angle for the remainder of our time down here. It was unlikely, but a girl could dream.

The wall adjacent to the mirrors was full of weapons: crossbows, spears, blades. The carpeted floor in the hallway didn't continue into the room. Instead, the entire flooring was matted. I gently pushed my heels into the foam, testing its cushiness. There wasn't any fancy workout equipment. There was just padded flooring. I supposed vampires didn't need to work out, but they did need to spar.

"We should get started. There's a bathroom in the

back," he said, pointing to a little wooden door hidden in the corner. "Put these on," he added, tossing me what looked like scraps of fabric.

With the flick of a wrist, I pulled them open: a black sports bra with a crisscrossed back—identical to the one I was already wearing—and black spandex shorts that seemed more like underwear than outerwear.

"You're kidding," I said, tearing my eyes away from the skimpy outfit. There was no way that I was going to wear this in *public*.

"Change quickly; we have a lot of work to do," he said.

"And why exactly do I have to wear *this*? Can't I just wear what I have on? It's flexible," I said, dropping into squats to emphasize my movement capabilities.

The grin on his face was more than enough evidence that he'd force me into these clothes anyway, yet I continued my mini workout routine, hoping I'd convince him that modern-day clothing was appropriate attire for workout buddies. While I wasn't the best fitness partner when I was human, I was still smart enough to know that items easily passable as lingerie didn't belong in the gym.

"Those won't do."

"But why?" I asked, ceasing my routine.

"Three reasons: one, you need to be able to see your body move," he said as he flicked up his pointer finger. "Two, you need to be free of restrictions. And three, everyone loves a good distraction. To determine your gift, you must be tested. To be tested, you must wear this attire. You'll understand as the day progresses."

Two and three received their own corresponding fingers as though it provided ample emphasis. Jasik spoke with a matter-of-fact tone, one he used at almost all times when we discussed the life of a vampire. I honestly believed that *he* believed everything he said would one day change the world—or at least be of great importance. They were just clothes. Though I wasn't sure what the big deal was, I gave up my argument and sulked into the bathroom.

I whined as I emerged, and even though Jasik was busily prepping an array of weaponry on a side table, I kept my frown plastered on my face. Good thing my mother was wrong when she said the longer I held it, the more likely it was to stick around forever. Though I had learned that the hard way.

When I was nine, she spent all night working a spell

that actually left my skin wrinkled for a week. The drop of my cheeks sparked enough fear to stop me from crying when I wasn't allowed a toy after leaving the market. I hoped my new vampire family would be slightly less literal.

I shifted from foot to foot and exhaled loudly. I felt ridiculous in my new workout uniform, and just in case Jasik wasn't aware of my frustration, I felt the need to make it extra evident. My blatant behavior caused him to grin, but his eyes didn't stray from the table.

Giving up, I walked over to the wall and slid my finger across the blade of a shiny silver… sword? I didn't know. Having a curved tip and being maybe two or three feet long, it seemed too small to be a sword, yet too long to be a dagger. But it was pretty, and it made me miss my katana. The mirrored blade ended in a black handle with swirling silver lines that seemed to glitter. The tip of the handle had a metallic stone. I rubbed my finger over the smooth surface. I pulled it from the wall, my palm firmly grasping it in place.

"Beautiful," Jasik said. I tore my eyes away from my newfound toy to look at him. He stared back, admiring, and I wondered if his word had more meaning than the weapon deserved.

I glanced at myself in the full-length mirrors. The clothes snugged tightly against my body, emphasizing each muscular curve—curves I was sure had formed *after* my transformation, and the blade gave my look an edge I'd never seen before. I looked fierce, dangerous. I turned and clenched my hand tighter around the blade's handle; my arm muscles obeyed the command, forming tight lines and bulging threateningly.

Jasik stepped behind me, placing a hand atop my own, and turned the blade. "Hold it like this," he said.

I was painfully aware of his proximity. His breath was cool on my bared back. I turned my head and met his eyes, letting his fingers linger. Shivers shot through my body when his skin lightly brushed against mine.

I said nothing—afraid to break the moment, yet terrified to let it continue.

How did he have such control over me? But more importantly, why did I let it happen? As if reading my thoughts, he pulled away, clearing his throat and returning to the table of weapons.

"That's a Celtic seax," he said, fiddling with things atop the table. "The handle has a very powerful crystal:

the hematite. It's believed that the hematite protects warriors in battle, so this particular stone holds great value to Hunters. I've had it since I was a child. It was my father's." He turned to face me, holding a small dagger, swirling it around in his hand while he spoke. "It's been restored, but if you like it, I want you to have it," he said.

"What? No. I can't. It's a family heirloom. I couldn't take this," I said, yet I kept my fingers firmly around the handle. I wanted to give it back, but letting go felt *wrong*.

He chuckled. "I suppose it is, but no one has used it for quite some time. I'd rather have it be of use than collecting dust." He paused before adding, "I want you to have it. Please."

I looked at the blade, raising it and resting the tip on my free palm. I moved my arms up and down. It was light—too light. Would it even be effective? How hard was it to kill a vampire, anyway?

"Would this work to kill a Rogue?" I asked.

"Most definitely. It's made of a strong metal. I've used it myself."

I nodded. "Okay, I mean, if you're sure." I wanted it. I didn't know why, but I was drawn to it. I *had* to have it.

I imagined myself twirling the weapon around me. I watched it slice through the necks of the Rogues I sought.

"Great, and I have a scabbard," he said, setting down the dagger and walking across the room to a cabinet. A scabbard? "I made this to fit on one's back," he said, opening the cabinet door and grabbing what I assumed was the scabbard. It looked like a sheath had been sewn into the back of my sports bra—minus the front cover up. Not surprisingly so, it was all black, but it had a crisscrossed back that lined up with my top. "You'll need to practice sliding your blade in and out, but in time, you should easily access it."

He tightened the arms on the scabbard with ease. "Turn around," he said, and I eagerly obeyed.

I set the seax on the table and slid my arms into the holes. It fit as if it were meant for me. I stepped away from Jasik and admired myself in the mirrors, turning my head to the side, trying to see where it rested on my back. The straps seamlessly fell into place with my sports bra.

I grabbed the seax from the table and mimicked Jasik's twirly maneuver, which was easier than I anticipated. I was used to twirling my katana, but the weight of the seax was different. It was as if I had to re-learn how to ride a bike.

Feeling daring, I flipped the blade upward in a twirling motion before yanking it down, hoping my aim would come as quickly as my weapon-twirling.

Only it didn't.

I dropped the blade as it sliced down my back, the metal cool, formidable. The strap of my top snagged on the blade, and the metal sliced through. I felt the blade enter muscle. I cried out, falling to the ground as it dug deeper into my back. I landed on my knees in a thump, and Jasik dropped to my side, catching me before I landed fully on the floor.

He grabbed the seax, which had nestled itself into my lower back, before it could cut deeper or sever my spine. Instinctively, I reached back, attempting to grab onto the handle and pull it from my body. I could only lift my arm a few inches before searing pain shot through me.

For the first time since I had willingly joined a coven of vampires, I thought I was going to die. I had survived countless vampire attacks, a birth rite that inflicted power too great for a mortal being to withstand, and a Rogue attack. Nothing had seemed worthy of taking my life—

except me. I would lose my life to a moment of self-inflicted stupidity.

"It's okay. You'll be okay," he said.

I screamed and dug my fingers into his skin as he pulled the seax from my back. The smell of blood filled the room, momentarily distracting me from the pain in my back.

"You'll heal in just a few min—" he said as the wound on my back began to heat and tingle. The pain left almost as quickly as it came, and I sank into a slumped position. I swallowed the knot in my throat and looked over my shoulder at the wall-to-wall mirrors behind us. The wound was gone.

"I thought I was going to die," I said. I had many close calls when patrolling the grounds near my home, but none had left me feeling so helpless. Here, I didn't have my coven to heal or protect me. I only had Jasik and his coven—most of whom didn't even want me here.

"That's not possible," he said, staring at my back.

"What?" For the first time since we had met, I was afraid of him. I was afraid of the uncertainty in his eyes.

"She used her shield on me this morning," he said. I

bobbed my head between Jasik and the spot he was staring at on the mirror, which wasn't aligned with my reflection.

I began pulling away from him, but he grabbed onto my arm. My pulse quickened. Was I actually going to die? I didn't understand his look of distrust.

"Let me go," I said.

"You just healed, Avah." He glanced down at me. He was conflicted. His eyes betrayed his feelings. I could hear his heart pounding as he attempted to control his breathing. Hard lines formed around his concerned eyes. But was he concerned for me? Or the mysterious visitor behind the mirror?

"Vampires are supposed to heal," I said in a sad attempt to brush off his fear. I pulled against his hold, but his centuries of built-up strength seemed to harden into stone.

"No, you *healed*. Not like a vampire. Like a healer." He glanced back to the mirror, and in a quick motion, he brought his other arm up and pinned me to the floor, eliminating the space between us. I squirmed beneath him, but he pushed me harder into the foam mat.

Fear erupted within me, and I resorted to begging.

"Jasik, please. I—I..." I didn't know what to say. The only vampire in the coven who cared for me now glared at me with newfound distrust. The others had already deemed me unworthy and were clearly out for blood.

"I'm sorry, Avah. Don't fight back. I won't hurt you." He spoke barely above a whisper. I was sure he was hoping the beings behind the mirror hadn't heard him. His fangs lengthened, and his irises glowed. "If I don't, *she* will—and she'll hurt you." Without warning, he slid his fangs into my neck.

I pushed against him, using all of my strength, screaming as he slowly drank. His fangs felt no differently than the seax's deathly encounter only moments earlier.

My nails against his skin drew blood. The smell of it was intoxicating, and slowly, the dull ache in my neck began to fade. My fangs lengthened. Seeing a way out, I turned my head, further exposing my neck but enough to bite into his shoulder.

I savagely tore at his skin, but he didn't flinch. As I pulled away, his skin glowed and healed. Weakening from blood loss, I released his arms from my grip.

"Please," I begged breathlessly.

He released my pinned arms, shifting his weight so that his body blocked my view of the mirrors. He lowered his free arm to my bare side, tracing circular, soothing patterns on my skin with his thumb. His gentle caress was comforting.

He pulled back, staring into my eyes. His irises were a shade of neon I hadn't seen before. They were brighter than when he'd used his magic, and the color was speckled with blackness. His eyes spoke of a hunger he wouldn't dare speak of. His gaze drifted to my mouth, and briefly, he leaned toward me. Ever so slightly, his lips brushed against mine but stopped short of forming the intimate connection.

He returned his mouth to my neck and suckled. My fangs dug into his lower neck, missing his artery, but getting a mouthful of blood, nonetheless. I heard a distant rustle, and the door to the room slammed open. The wind shifted.

"Enough," she said, an order he could not refuse. His fangs retracted, and he pushed himself off the ground, holding my limp body in his arms. The blackness within his eyes vanished as he stood, and he looked at his priestess. "What did you feel?" she continued.

"Her power is great. She would, Milady, be an invaluable asset. We can't lose this power to another."

Her eyes drifted to where I was cradled—unable to move even as my body began to heal. She watched me as she decided my fate. I prayed she would hand down leniency.

As much as I hated Jasik for what he'd done, I couldn't deny that I understood his motives. I too would have stopped at nothing to protect my coven.

"Train her. Make her an asset, or it will be your head," she said before leaving the room. The other vampires that had followed her into the room took heed and swiftly guarded her exit. The door closed, and we were alone.

"Avah, I'm so sorry," he said as he wiped a tear from my cheek. "We had to be sure the threat Lillie foresaw wasn't you."

I swallowed hard, my throat painfully dry. My head throbbed.

"Your wounds are healing, but you must drink," he said. "You're weak."

"They're… watching," I choked out.

He shook his head. "Not anymore." His thumb

traced circles on my temple.

I slowly nodded, my neck stiff. I reached an arm out to point at the mirrors, but it fell.

"They're not there. I promise. Listen," he said. "Listen with your heart."

My heart? I had no idea how to listen with my heart. I could barely keep my eyes open. They threatened to flutter shut with every word.

"Drink," he said. "Please." He pulled my broken body into a sitting position and rested my head against his neck.

"My room," I said weakly. I wouldn't be able to stay awake much longer, and I needed to know that I was safely tucked away in my room—anything that separated me from *them*. I felt like a fool for trusting him, and now that I needed him, I felt sick. "Please," I said as my eyelids became too heavy to bear.

When I opened them again, I was in my room. I didn't know how much time had passed—minutes, days, weeks; it all felt the same. My body ached even though my wounds had closed before his priestess had even left the room.

Jasik stood over me, and in a swift motion, he took

off his shirt and dropped it to the floor. Effortlessly, he lowered himself onto the bed, lying beside me. His forehead brushed against mine as he propped me up against his bare torso. His eyes were once again wide and speckled with black. He lowered my lips to his neck, and I bit down, taking long, deep gulps of blood, welcoming its sweet embrace.

He groaned, turning so I straddled him. As his blood filled me, I got stronger. I continued drinking, unable to stop—even after I no longer felt the twinge of weakness. I sucked harder, taking in every drop.

When I no longer needed to feed, but still drank, I began to feel. I felt everything he was. I felt the encaged animal inside of him, I felt the power his years had given him, and I felt his affinity for healing. His blood, full of emotions, told his story. I felt the pain he had once endured when he lost his family. I felt his love for his high priestess. I felt his fear of the Rogue vampire race. I felt his sorrow for the witches he had killed. And finally, I felt his love. An abundance of love nestled deep within him. A love so pure, so true. A love he had never unleashed. A love he was slowly beginning to unravel.

I sucked harder, hoping to look deeper. He unlocked

the door to the night we met. His attraction was immediate. His disgust with himself after leaving me to die was overwhelming.

I was brought back to reality as his fingertips tickled my lower back. When I was no longer digging into his past, he ran a hand up my back until it settled against my neck, the other finding its place by my hip, grinding my body against his. His fingers scratched at my sports bra, careful not to rip the straps.

I lost my control. I knew this was wrong, but I was driven by pure animal instinct. I felt the need, the hunger, nestled deep within me. The animal inside was itching to be released.

"Avah," he whispered. I released his neck to meet his eyes and was shocked at what I saw: vulnerability. I knew he would completely give himself to me, if only I'd ask. I could take his body, his blood, his power... his life. His fate sat at my fingertips. He leaned forward, placing his lips against mine, inviting, daring... begging.

And I faltered. I gave in, breaking under the pressure, the need.

My body curved into his, and I noticed how we fit together perfectly. I hadn't expected to find my match in a vampire, but as he wrapped his arms around me, the world became hazy just as it had when we stood together in his bedroom earlier today.

The space intimate.

We were connected beyond the physical. Each time his hands brushed against my skin, each time he spoke my name, showing just a hint of an English accent, I felt as though I lived for him.

He brushed his lips teasingly against mine, urging me on to make the first move. Parting my lips, I opened my mouth, fangs throbbing at my need. His breathing became heavy as he pushed against me. I bit into my lower lip, dragging my teeth against it until releasing it back in place. I dug my fingers into his arms as he reached down and grabbed my thighs. I grazed my tongue against his lips before quickly pulling away. I leaned into his neck, the marks from my earlier bite gone, and took a deep breath.

Old Spice.

He gasped as I brushed my fangs against his neck, a thin layer of blood trickling onto my pillow. His skin glowed around the cut and then healed, eliminating any trace of my mark.

His fingers dug into my skin as I licked the leftover line of blood away. He groaned long and deep and drew his face back to mine.

Satisfied with teasing, I pushed my lips against his, welcoming their smooth caress. His tongue playfully slipped into my mouth, and I returned the gesture. I pulled him against me, needing to experience every inch of him

My hands found his arms and chest, rubbing against the curves, emphasizing every ridge of muscle. The kiss seemed to go on forever, and I accepted that fate— frightened at the thought that it might end, that I might lose him. I urged him on, but he pulled back, glancing at my neck with fangs peeking out past his opened mouth. Our chests heaved as we gasped for air. He glanced from my neck to my eyes, asking for permission.

I hesitated, the seconds drawing by slowly as I considered his request, but he patiently waited. Slowly, I nodded. He rolled over so that he was on top of me. His fangs pierced my skin quickly, cleanly, and I moaned in sheer pleasure. The searing pain that once burned my insides to my core was gone, and in its stead was a wash of ecstasy.

I had no idea what my actions tonight would bring with them tomorrow, but I didn't care.

There was only Jasik.

There was only me.

There was only blood.

CHAPTER
EIGHT

I WOKE TO the slow, steady beat of his heart. Careful to not wake him, I glanced down. Fully clothed. I don't know why I was surprised. I remembered everything from the night before. I remembered my fear and distrust. I remembered my hunger, my need for him. I remembered his equally powerful need for me. I remembered it all. And I certainly would have remembered sex.

I bit my lower lip. I almost had sex with him, with the man I had only begun to trust, to know.

I turned to face him. He slept on his back, his face away from mine. The blanket was by our feet, and in the heat of the night, he hadn't redressed. His chiseled torso was exposed to lingering eyes, and I felt mine pausing far too long.

I jerked my head away so that I stared at the ceiling, and then I squeezed my eyes shut and bit down hard on my lip. He shifted, the quick motion of my discomfort the obvious culprit.

Why was I so worried he'd wake? It wasn't as if we'd never see each other again. Our relationship passed one-night stand the moment I walked into the house—and I was sure we'd had the vampires' version of sex. At least, I felt dirty thinking about everything we'd done.

I slowly moved my right leg so that it was hanging off the bed, hovering over the floor. I shifted ever so slightly, maneuvering until I stood. I released the breath I held.

"Sneaking away?" he said before turning on his bedside light.

"Creep much?" I faced him, forced a smile, and shrugged. I felt like my mother had just caught me stealing cookies before dinner. That feeling couldn't possibly be a good start to a relationship.

He smiled and licked his lips, an innocent move that shouldn't have felt so... provocative.

Truth is, I didn't want to leave. I wanted to wake in

his arms night after night. I wanted to see that face, hear that voice, each and every evening. But giving in was harder than I had imagined. I needed to know that I still wanted this relationship when my life wasn't in danger, and at that moment, the lingering feeling of his lips on mine made it hard to concentrate on what I *really* needed. And all I needed was to learn how to track and kill a select group of Rogues.

"I think it's better if we have some space." The words came out harsher than I intended, and the pain they caused him reflected in his eyes. "I mean, I just think, you know, I think it'd be better if we—"

"I understand, Avah. You do not need to explain."

In a swift motion, he stood, pulled on a t-shirt, and walked to the end of the bed. His fingertips trailed the footboard as he slowly approached me.

"I betrayed your trust. You need time. I understand." He spoke softly and smiled.

I looked away, unsure of what to say. He was right. He did betray me. The betrayal hurt, but I understood. I would have done the same had the roles been reversed. I knew of the importance of a coven—and your vow to them. I couldn't tell him the truth. I couldn't tell him the reason I needed space was because I wasn't scared of him; I was scared of me, of my feelings.

He eliminated the space between us. With his fingertips, he pulled my hair behind my ear, letting his fingers linger on my earlobe before bringing his thumb down the curve of my jawline.

"You're so beautiful," he said, and my breath caught. I could feel my heart pounding in my chest, and I was sure he heard it, too. I felt my cheeks heat as blood rushed toward them, and I instinctively looked away, embarrassed as my cheeks grew hot. With his fingers below my chin, he brought my gaze back to meet his.

"I'm so sorry, Avah, but if you'll let me, in time, I will prove that I am worthy of your trust. I give you my word." His voice was sincere, and I had no doubt that his word meant everything to him.

He lowered his hand and stepped back. His eyes lowered briefly, and I found myself wetting my lips.

"If you need me, I'll be across the hall," he said, and I smiled. Jasik may have been a lot of things, but unchivalrous would never be one of them.

I HAD HOPED being alone in my room would give me a sense of escape. Instead, I felt trapped. I paced the floor, watching as the walls closed in around me. I had to get out of here.

I closed my bedroom door behind me and sprinted down the hall. As I turned to take the stairs, the door to Amicia's bedroom opened. One of her guards, wearing only black leather pants, stepped out. Before he quickly closed the door behind him, I glanced inside. Amicia lay nude on her bed, feeding from her other guard. He moaned as she ran her hand up and down the length of his torso. I looked away, embarrassed. The guard cleared his throat. Two lines of dried blood caked his neck.

I ignored his look of curiosity and ran down the stairs, rushing through the front door. The air was moist. My feet pounded against the frost-covered ground. In my haste, I hadn't changed. I didn't care that I was running away barefoot or in clothes that covered no more than undergarments. I just knew I needed to get away. I needed space.

The air washed away my guilt, my fear, my hatred. I felt at peace again. Calmed by Mother Earth. I slowed until I was only walking through the brush. Twigs snapped beneath my feet. I smiled as I reached my arm out to let the pine needles scratch my skin. I knew I wasn't in northern California anymore, but I found pieces of home everywhere I looked.

The woods opened to the water's edge. A small creek that dribbled down what had to be the world's smallest waterfall and into a stream sat before me. I fell to my knees, ignoring the squishing sensation I felt as my legs burrowed into the cold, hard mud. I scooped the clear water into my palms and took a sip.

It tasted like water—only better. It was crisp, clean. I swished the cool liquid around my mouth, lathering my tongue before swallowing it down. The sensation trickled down my throat and into my stomach. I could feel the cold in the air. I could feel the icy water, but the feeling didn't bother me. I wondered what the new parts of me could withstand. I ran my fingertips across the almost-still stream.

Twigs broke in the distance, and I jumped to my feet. My stomach grew uneasy and made it almost impossible to concentrate on the sounds of the woods.

Though I couldn't see them—yet—I knew they watched me where they stood. I slowly took a step backward, still scanning the forest. I released deep breaths, forcing my heartbeat to slow.

I needed the predators watching me to consider me a threat. I was not their prey.

I refused to back down. After all, killing these Rogues would be good practice for the ones I really wanted. I stood tall, threateningly. My hands were clenched at my sides. In a final attempt to scare them away, I lowered my fangs and released a low growl. The only vampires I had encountered were those in my new coven. They saw me as a threat, but made no move to eliminate it. I wasn't sure how other vampires would react to me—and I wasn't sure I wanted to know.

They emerged from the tree line. There were three. All men. They were strong, old. I sensed their age the moment they appeared. Older vampires transmitted a powerful scent. It smelled of ash and death. These vampires wore bloodstained clothes. Their skin was dark with dirt. As I assessed their physique (and my survival rate), they continued approaching me. They splashed through the stream, walking toward me with a confidence that shook me to my core.

I cursed under my breath for not bringing a weapon. When they were only feet away, their fangs lowered, and they charged. I stood my ground. I would not falter. The first approached me from the front. A fatal mistake. I lunged forward just as he became within arm's reach. I twisted to the side, my arms before me. I spun around until I stood behind him. My hands wrapped around his neck and jerked. His neck snapped. I knotted my fingers in his hair, digging my nails against his scalp, and pressed my free hand against his shoulder. I yanked his head up while pushing his body down. He tumbled to the ground.

I spun around, facing the final two attackers. They no longer pursued me. Instead, they stood, jaws ajar in disbelief. I lifted my right arm in display. The vampire's head hung from my fingers, and I tossed the member toward his friends. His head rolled to a stop at their feet.

I took their moment of uncertainty for my advantage. I raised my arms to my sides, my fingers flicking them toward me in a daring move. My eyebrow arched, and my lips curved into a smile.

"Well, boys. Let's dance," I said.

The larger of the two growled. His muscles tightened as he threw his arms out to his sides and curled his fingers. His thick nails lengthened, and his face morphed into a disfigured monster. His skin paled and fell sunken against his bones. His ears grew to points as veins protruded from his forehead. His beady eyes turned black, and I took a step backward, unable to look away from the monstrosity before me.

The vampires I grew up learning about truly did exist. The creature before me unleashed the demon within him—and I instigated it.

He released a deep bellow as his limbs began tearing through his clothes. He continued to grow until he towered over me.

The other vampire had not changed. Instead, he ran toward me, his feet slapping against the water. He slammed into me, and I flew backward. I crashed into a tree, its branch piercing my core. I cried out, frantically trying to relieve the pressure. I gasped for air and hacked up blood as my lungs filled. I brought my legs back and placed the soles of my feet against the thick trunk. Pushing against the base of the tree, I slowly began sliding myself off. With the tree no longer holding my weight, I fell to the ground in a thump.

The vampire stood beside me, laughing as I attempted to stand. I thrashed around, inevitably failing to hold my weight. He stepped away as the monstrous leader grabbed me by the neck and lifted me until we were eye level. My legs swayed in the air as I tried to fight him off.

His hand slipped to the back of my head, yanking my neck to a more revealing position. My breath came unevenly. The blood that coated the wound on my stomach turned thick as my body slowly healed from the damage done.

"*Incendia*," I breathed. But nothing happened. I was too weak—weak enough to lose my magic. A single tear slid down my cheek. The vampire leaned in, inhaling dramatically. He was only a fang's length from me now. I used what little strength I had left, pushing forward, falling into his arms.

He was startled. It was a move no one would have expected. The move left me vulnerable and displayed a show of affection Rogue vampires could not comprehend. I threw my head back, lowered my fangs, and dug into his neck. His blood soared through me. His strength healed my wounds and left me stronger, more alert than ever before.

I drank until there was nothing left. At some point, he had fallen into my arms. I held his limp body, his disfigured disguise melting away as he slowly shriveled. I tossed his body to the ground. His friend had gone, leaving his leader to die.

I licked my lips and ran my hands over my healed stomach. I closed my eyes as I looked toward the sky and inhaled deeply. I found him almost immediately. His heart sputtered beneath his chest; his feet slammed against the ground as he tried to escape me. I ran toward him, catching him within seconds.

I grabbed the back of his neck and tossed him into the air. He tumbled to a stop, quickly moving to his feet, facing me. I slowly walked toward him. I eliminated the space between us, and he fell to his knees in a pleading position. He had given up. I was surprised by his actions.

The wind shifted as someone approached. I looked up and found Jasik watching me. He said nothing, as if he were giving me permission to decide the vampire's fate. I turned to face the enemy again. He was on his feet. His eyes were cold, hard. I knew he'd kill again. I wouldn't let him kill another. I wouldn't let him murder any more witches.

I raised my right arm and allowed my magic to flow within me. It coursed through my veins. With regained strength, I knew I could control my magic again. I smiled.

"*Incendia!*" I said. I spoke powerfully, confidently. I watched the flame spark and strengthen until he was covered in the fire. He screamed as it overwhelmed him. He tried to stand as if he planned to run but instead fell to the ground. It took only seconds for the steady beat of his heart to slow to a stop. The fire remained kindled until there was nothing but ash.

I smelled Jasik approach—his musky scent followed wherever he went—but I didn't take my eyes off the vampire's remains. Jasik stood behind me, rubbing his hand along my arm until it rested in my palm.

"Let's clean this up," he said as he squeezed my hand tightly.

"There are more," I said.

"Yes, Malik will take care of them."

I faced Jasik, tearing my eyes away from the Rogue's remains. "One was different, deformed."

Jasik dropped my hand; wrinkles of surprise briefly danced across his forehead.

"What?"

"That's not possible," he said, looking in the direction where the other bodies lay.

"What? What's not possible?" I asked, frustrated.

He ignored me and instead walked into the brush, pushing away branches until he found the creature's remains.

"You killed an elder Rogue?" Jasik asked.

"Is that what that was?" I asked, shrugging.

"Do not dismiss this, Avah. It's an incredible accomplishment for such a young Hunter. Even I have never managed such a task."

"He was stronger, but he was stupid. He was too confident. It left his side vulnerable," I said, looking at the fresh wounds on his neck.

"I do not know what is more flabbergasting: the fact that you alone killed an elder Rogue or that you fed from one while he was alive. How do you feel?"

"I—I don't know. Good. Strong."

"As you should. Elder Rogues have lived for thousands of years. They were the first vampires. His power, his strength, was in his blood, which now courses through your veins."

"So what does that mean?" I asked, rubbing my hands against my clothes, hoping to wipe away the stench of death.

"You'll be much stronger. Temporarily, of course. His power was not meant to be yours and will not stay within you forever. But this is a great achievement."

"There was something different about his scent. I could tell he was old. And then he just… changed. He became a monster—one of the monsters the elders of my own coven warned me about," I said, losing myself in my thoughts.

"Elder Rogues have lived without their humanity, without their souls, for thousands of years. Depravation in that extent leaves long-lasting effects."

"I had no idea something like this existed," I said.

"That's because very few survive an encounter with such a powerful Rogue. We still are unsure of how many even exist."

"It was just luck," I said, and I found myself focusing on the world around me, listening for any signs of danger lurking. I was the most powerful I had ever been in my life, but I felt weak, terrified, incapable of protecting myself against the dangers of this new world.

CHAPTER
NINE

A WEEK HAD passed before the coven's priestess asked to see me. I was surprised she hadn't insisted on the meeting sooner; news of my kills had spread like wildfire through the coven, but it was quickly forgotten. Jasik had assured me no harm would come. Hunters were meant to kill Rogues. But he still spoke with a hint of fear. I wasn't sure if he was afraid for me or of me.

"She requested we meet alone," I said as Jasik followed me to her door. Around us, the vampires hustled down the hall, busily putting final touches on house decorations for tonight's event. The announcement of vampires from other covens attending the annual New Year's Eve masquerade ball put everyone on edge, but thankfully, they paid me no mind to me. I was finally beginning to feel like I belonged here.

"Yes, I'll be in my room, preparing for tonight's festivities." He smiled reassuringly.

I nodded. "No training today, right? Big party and all."

"No time, but we'll pick up again tomorrow."

"Okay, good. I don't want to take too much time off," I said as we reached Amicia's office.

"Don't worry so much, Avah. You're a few hundred years too young for worry lines," he said with a sly grin.

I smiled as I knocked on her office door. Jasik turned to leave as I slipped inside once given permission. I remembered the way her Hunters stood before: tall with one arm resting behind their backs and the other at their sides. I mimicked that stance.

"Good evening, Avah."

I nodded. "Milady."

"Tell me about your transition. Jasik has been updating me nightly about your training. He has assured me you're a quick study. Do you feel you're coming into your new life and abilities?"

"Yes, Milady. Jasik has been very helpful."

"So it seems. He informed me that you're already

trained in combat and that you'll be quite valuable once you learn what it truly means to be a vampire."

"Thank you," I said, though I wasn't sure what she meant by *truly* being a vampire.

"I heard of your hunting in our woods, and I wanted to thank you for eliminating a nearby threat. Rogues rarely come this close to the manor."

"You're welcome," I said.

"I was delighted to hear that you went hunting on your own. Do you feel you're prepared to venture out again?"

I wasn't sure what to say. I realized Jasik must've given her a slightly different version of the day's events. I'm sure he neglected to tell her I was running from my feelings and our feeding.

She crossed her arms over her chest and leaned back in her chair, awaiting my response.

"I don't know. There's still a lot I don't know." Was she planning to send me out on my own? Did she think I was capable of looking after myself so there was no need to keep me around?

"Yes, there is. The Hunters of this house are highly skilled and have been directed to do whatever it takes to ensure you are prepared for this life."

"Thank you."

"I trust you will come to me if you have any doubts," she said.

Doubts about what? Staying here? Training with vampires? *Being* a vampire? Did I even have a choice in the matter?

"Doubts, Milady?"

"Yes. Doubts." She spoke confidently as if I knew exactly what she was referring to.

"Sure—yes. I'll come to you if I need anything," I said.

"Very well. I hope you'll join us this evening, Avah. Our masquerade ball is a cherished event. Members and priestesses of covens all around the world are invited to join us in welcoming the new year."

"I wouldn't miss it." I plastered a wide smile on my face. It was forced, but at this point, it was getting uncomfortable.

"Have you anything to wear?"

I thought about the racks of clothing in my closet. I was sure there was something in there suitable for a ball.

"If not, inform Jasik. He will take care of it."

"Yes, Milady."

She smiled at me, and I realized that was the first time I had ever seen her smile. It was small, but genuine.

"That's all," she said, looking down at the papers scattered across her desk.

"Good evening, Milday," I said as I turned to leave.

"Oh, Avah," she said, and I faced her with the doorknob in hand. "I shouldn't have to tell you how important your presence will be this evening. You may have only spent a short time here with us, but your... *creation* has been news. Everyone will be watching you, seeing where your allegiance lies. I've been watching you since you've arrived. I know you've formed relations with the Hunters of this house. We have welcomed you into our home, Avah. Like humans, status is everything in our culture. They will be watching you. Give them a show."

I said nothing. I simply nodded. I understood what she asked of me. I needed to choose a side, and I needed to make my decision known. I needed to showcase my power, her weapon.

I returned to my room in a daze. Was I ready to showcase my power, to seriously choose a side? I closed my bedroom door behind me and switched on the light.

A sexy black evening gown hung from one of the posts of my bed. I walked over to it, running my hand across the silky fabric. With a thigh-high slit and a thick, one-sided strap, I felt provocative just thinking about wearing the gown. The top was a low princess cut, and most of the gown was sheer. I hadn't realized becoming a vampire meant showing this much skin.

A simple black mask with a violet shimmer. Under the mask was a note from Jasik: *For you.* It was simple, direct, but oddly arousing. I dropped the note, grabbed the dress, and walked toward the mirror. I felt like a princess as I pushed the sheer gown against me.

I glanced at the time: it was nearly eleven in the evening. I frantically showered, applied dark eye makeup, and styled my hair in a sweeping updo with soft curls. I didn't want my long hair to distract anyone from the gorgeous gown, which meant I had to bare even more skin.

I slipped into the form-fitting dress and tied the mask on. My violet irises burned brightly against the dark colors of the mask and dress. I was certain Jasik chose this dress specifically for that reason. I felt more beautiful than I'd ever felt before. Smiling as I left my room for the party, I thought of how badly I wanted to see Jasik's reaction to me in this dress.

The double doors opened as I approached, and I was greeted by two vampires. Though their faces were hidden behind masks, I recognized their stance, their eyes, their smell. They were part of Amicia's entourage. I guessed their duties went beyond her chambers.

"Welcome, Miss Taylor," they said in unison. I smiled.

I gasped as I entered the room. The ceiling was adorned with a shimmery finish, fitting beautifully into the starry night. Iridescent streams of fabric dangled along the walls, hiding the wood frames. A floor-to-ceiling tree sat in the corner, decorated with sparkling red and silver ornaments and white twinkling lights. A champagne waterfall sat along another wall, nestled between two towers of glasses. Its bubbling, sweet scent tickled my nose. A dozen circular tables with fitted, sheer white table cloths were scattered around the room. Wordless music played from hidden speakers. Members of my new coven huddled in corners, busily gossiping with vampires and priestesses from other covens, while others danced in the middle of the room. The grand hall was utterly breathtaking.

I walked to the champagne bar and was handed a full glass. The others around me watched as I sipped my drink, whispering secrets under their breath. I smiled but was left facing backs. I wondered if I would ever be welcomed in this house.

"You look beautiful," a voice said from behind me.

I turned to find a masked figure with icy-blue irises and a boyish grin. I unsuccessfully fought my eyes as they drifted down his frame. His black suit and tie made him look breathtakingly handsome. His black mask was simple with only speckles of light blue, making his eyes shine even brighter.

"Even in the midst of this chaos, you're still easy to find," he added.

"I can't imagine why," I said with a grin. "My eyes betray my identity even behind a mask."

"Your eyes betray your beauty, Avah, and nothing less," he said, eyes intense. My breath caught.

I looked away, drawing my gaze to the dance floor. My eyes rested on the vampires in masks before me. Many laughed, pulling their mates closer. Others fed in the corners. Some smiled for pictures, displaying two perfect points.

"What do you see?" Jasik asked as he glanced down at me.

What did I see? I saw potential enemies in the newcomer vampires. I saw members of my own coven who didn't trust me. But when I looked at Jasik, I saw something different. He didn't hate or fear me. He gave me a chance. As I turned to face him again, his difference, his beauty, mocked the idea behind what I saw.

"What do you see?" I countered.

His lips briefly curved into a small smile before disappearing into a hard line. The seconds he waited to answer hung in the air. His face bore his typical features, that of a man thinking too hard about the words he chose. "I see you," he finally said.

I stared back and swallowed hard, fighting back the emotional flood that threatened to erupt within me.

He leaned in, brushing his lips against my ear, and added, "All I ever see is you."

Pulling back, he softly slid his thumb down the curve of my jawline.

"You carry your soul in your hands and hold it out

for the world to see, and all I want is to pull it close to me and cover it with my own. All I want is to take this fragile part of you that you so generously share with the world and protect it. Shade it from the sun yet hide it from darkness," he said, dropping his hand from my jaw and taking a step backward. He cleared his throat as if his honesty even surprised himself.

"Jasik," I whispered. I began to take a step forward but stopped myself. He smiled and held his hand out to me.

"May I have this dance?" he asked.

I placed my fingers in his palm. "Always."

He whisked me onto the floor and pulled me close to him. I admired how our bodies curved into each other as if it were our natural placement. We quickly fell in step, and at some point in the dance, I lost track of time and song. There was only us and the way our heartbeats matched. I closed my eyes and placed my ear against his chest, listening to the rhythmic beats. The world beyond us slipped away, and I willingly let it go, hoping that this moment would last a lifetime.

But a lifetime turns to forever when you're immortal, and songs seem to ignore one's pleas after just a few minutes.

"May I cut in?" a voice said.

I lifted my head from Jasik's chest and opened my eyes to find Lillie beside us. Jasik's grip on my waist tightened as I began to pull away.

"Sure," I said with a smile.

Her smile widened as she grabbed Jasik's hand and pulled him to her.

I stared at the floor as I walked away. From the shadows, I watched as they danced, twirling in the same way Jasik and I had. Her pink, strapless gown clung tightly to her body and flowed down to the floor. She hid behind a matching pink mask that sparkled under the dim lighting. She was beautiful, and next to Jasik's towering stance, she seemed to fit together with him just as well as I had. My heart sank as she said something inaudible, and Jasik smiled down at her.

"Don't let her get to you," Malik said. I briefly glanced at him as he stepped beside me.

"She knows parts of him that I'll never know," I said, keeping my eyes on the two that twirled on the dance floor. The words escaped me, and as I said them, as I opened my heart to Malik, I instantly regretted it. I couldn't let him in the way I'd let Jasik capture my heart. Beneath the layers of lust, there was a sensible girl who knew this was wrong. I couldn't let myself love Jasik— even though I so badly wanted to.

"She knows only of his past," Malik replied, seemingly unaware of the battle within me. I looked up at him, but he spoke without meeting my gaze. Instead, with his hands clasped behind his back, he watched his brother and the girl. "But Jasik doesn't live for the past," he said, turning to face me. "And you are very much his future."

I hoped my many emotions didn't dance across my face. I knew of the vampires' distrust and hatred for me; I had never expected one—especially Jasik's brother—to acknowledge that there was something there, something between us. Something that could make Malik look past my Pagan ancestry and accept me. Jasik was all Malik had. I thought about my family and how I would do anything for them: fight, kill, die. Yet they did not grant the same allegiance to me. Malik's devotion to his brother was clear. I knew admitting his brother's feelings for me hurt him. And I knew, given the chance, Malik would have stolen the life Jasik bestowed upon me. And although every fiber of my being told me to fear him, to protect *my* life, I couldn't. My feelings for Jasik forced me to have feelings for Malik, too.

"My gift grants me the ability to see any future that affects my own, Avah. I want you to understand that," he said.

"I do," I said, confused.

"My brother's future affects mine, and your future affects his. Do you understand?"

I didn't speak. I didn't know what he wanted me to say.

He faced me, eyes hard. "Your obsession with the Rogues who tore your humanity away will be your demise. But more importantly, it will be Jasik's, too. His love for you has blinded him. He will stop at nothing to protect you, and that will leave him vulnerable. Do what you need to do to let it go. Move on. End your obsession. For Jasik."

He turned and walked away before I could speak. His long legs had effortlessly taken him to the middle of the room by the time I was able to process his warning. I fully understood his meaning: if I continued on this path, I would die—and I'd bring Jasik with me. Every fiber of my being was screaming, but I couldn't let it go. I had come too far to simply walk away from the fight now.

"But they're not worth it," I whispered to myself.

From across the room, I watched Malik pause, turn his head, and then straighten his stance before stopping where Jeremiah was wooing a group of girls.

I returned my gaze to the dance floor, watching as Jasik dropped Lillie's arms as the song ended. She begged for another dance. I didn't need super hearing to know that. Anyone would've guessed after watching her run her hands up and down his back as he tried to walk away, turning to pout when she realized he wasn't complying.

"Would you care to join me outside?" Jasik asked when he reached my side.

The air was cool on my cheeks, the wind misty; I licked the clustered water droplets forming on my lips and brushed my hands against my arms as if to fight back the cold. It was a habit I had yet to control. I dropped my arms, embarrassed.

I would never be good at being a vampire.

Jasik stepped ahead of me and stared at the moon. It shined brightly, illuminating patches of the ground. Shadows still hid the secrets of this house: the headstones for fallen members of the coven, gargoyles sworn to protect the manor, fountains and statues and runes—runes hidden under the mossy pathway, behind the stone walls, within the statues.

"There's a full moon tonight," he said, still staring at the sky. "We'd better stay within the gates," he added with a grin.

I smiled at his attempted humor and leaned against him. Resting my head against his chest, I closed my eyes and listened to the creatures of the night. I focused on them, on their heartbeats and fluttering wings. I focused on the way it sounded when they slithered. It was beautiful.

I wasn't sure how much time had passed when Jasik asked if I was ready to rejoin the party.

"Yeah, I'm ready," I said.

He closed the French doors as we entered the ballroom again. Vampires smiled at me as I walked past, and I found myself returning the gesture.

"Oh my goddess! I love your dress," a girl said. She smiled, her fangs hanging ever so slightly lower than canine teeth. Her blonde hair, white with age, was tied back into a tight bun. Her skin wrinkled in the corners of her eyes as she widened her smile.

"Thank you," I said, instinctively running my hands over the smooth edges of the gown. I glanced up, meeting Jasik's eyes. They smiled at me, and I blushed.

"You look beautiful. Your dress is gorgeous," I said. Her white gown sparkled as she swayed from side to side. Her dark brown eyes looked bleak against her silver mask.

"Thank you, Avah." My heart sunk as she said my name. I knew my status in the house wasn't unfamiliar to the guests, but it didn't change the way I felt when someone I had yet to meet knew who I was. "I was hoping I would have the opportunity to speak with you tonight. Your transition was quite intriguing. Never has a vampire of such authority blatantly disobeyed our laws," she said, her eyes lingering on Jasik. "By the way, this is a great ball, Jasik. As always."

"Thank you," he said firmly. "Milady has outdone herself once again."

"Seems she has," the woman said.

Someone pounded on the door—once, twice, thrice—and the room silenced. Malik was beside Jasik faster than I could turn to face them. No one spoke.

Instead, the Hunters sprang into action. Jeremiah's shield enveloped the house in a protective layer unwanted visitors couldn't break through. The few Hunters who accompanied their coven's vampires scurried to protect their priestesses.

Jasik grabbed my hand, and I followed the Hunters into the hallway that led to the front door. The knocking came again. I turned to Lillie, who stood beside me, her eyes glossy as she read the visitors' minds.

"They—they want to talk," she said, confusion filling her voice. "About Avah." She looked at me.

Jasik squeezed my hand, and my eyes met his.

"I need you to be prepared to fight," he said. "It will come to that, understand?"

I nodded.

"I won't be able to protect this coven… and you."

His words escaped his lips in a hushed tone. I knew it hurt him to say that he couldn't be there for me if I needed him.

"I don't need you to protect me," I said, pulling my hand from his grip. "I'm ready for this."

He paused momentarily, watching me, his eyes hard, distant. He then faced the door and nodded to Malik.

I held my breath as it creaked open. The Rogues stood before us. There were at least a few dozen. My breath caught as I assessed the threat level just as I had while patrolling the woods that lined our property in Shasta.

The leader stood in front, just feet away from the shielded border. He smiled when he saw me. His eyes trailed down my frame as he looked at me. He licked his lips, his blood-red irises shining brightly.

"I've waited centuries for you," he said, meeting my eyes. Jasik tensed beside me. "You're even more beautiful than I imagined."

"You're not welcomed here," Jasik said. "Leave now."

The Rogue vampires before us laughed at his leave-or-die scenario. We were severely outnumbered, and they knew it. Jeremiah's shield was all that stood between these fiends and the royalty attending our ball. I was sure they knew that, too. The protection of the priestesses here befell the Hunters of this house.

I knew Jeremiah would not be able to leave the house. The vampires inside were too important. His shield must stand. If he left the safety of his shield, he'd be put in unnecessary danger. The Rogues knew that.

That left four Hunters able to fight. We wouldn't survive.

"You must forgive my rather vulgar attempts to retrieve you, but when we discovered another prophetic witch was so close, we had to move quickly. Certainly, you understand."

My memories came crashing back in waves. The Rogues before me were undeniably familiar. We'd met before—on the night of my birth rite. Anger boiled in the pit of my gut. I began to shake in frustration as I clenched my fists.

Malik cleared his throat, breaking my concentration. I met his eyes, and he slowly shook his head. My eyes slowly trailed back to the Rogue before me.

"I have an offer for you. You for their lives."

"Never," Jasik interrupted.

The Rogue smiled. "Very well." He drew his arm back and slammed his fist against the shield. Jeremiah fell to the ground.

"Jeremiah!" Lillie yelled, falling to his aid. She ripped his mask off and cupped his face between her palms.

"I'm—I'm okay. Wind knocked out of me. That's

all."

When the vampire struck again, a few more joined him. Jeremiah cried out in pain as they slammed their fists against our shield. I could hear the partygoers begging to be spared. Where we stood, we were powerless. We had but only a few options: let me leave with them, risk a fight, or wait to die.

In a daze, I looked from the vampires to Jasik and from Jasik to where Jeremiah lay, thrashing in pain as the Rogue forced all of Jeremiah's strength into maintaining his shield. I knew it was only a matter of time before it fell.

I realized then that this coven needed me, but more importantly, I needed them. All of them. I needed the Hunters and their vast array of knowledge. I needed Amicia and her constant pushing, forcing me to see my worth. I needed Jasik, and he needed me.

In this moment, this vulnerable moment, as Jasik looked at me, his eyes begged for an answer. His coven would fall. Everything Jasik had fought for was being taken away before his eyes. The Rogues laughed as Jeremiah's shield shook under their immense strength. But in that moment, as he stared back at me, I knew what I needed to do.

When I became a vampire, he told me to accept what I was, and I stubbornly ignored him. But as the vampires that took me in would soon fall before me, I knew it was time to accept the truth: I was a vampire. The one thing I hated most in my human life. But I wasn't human anymore. I had to release my grasp on mortality and welcome my immortality.

I raised my right hand and shouted, "*Terra!*" The ground grumbled beneath our feet as I called upon earth. I maintained my vice-like grip and raised my left arm, shouting, "*Incendia!*" The vampires combusted before us. The leader was engulfed in flames. I pulled at the immortal power within me, tugging it until it wrapped me in a warm blanket. Power radiated off me. It pulsed within. I shouted my Latin incantations again, strengthening the fire on the Rogues. Those who stood in the distance ran, leaving those in the front to perish. The leader, now on his knees and leaning against the shield, met my gaze. I blinked, and he was gone, vanished into the darkness, but I knew, in time, he'd be back for me. He was strong, like the Rogue I'd fought in the woods. The flames I cast would only hurt him, not kill him.

I released the elements and fell to my knees. I rested my hands atop Jeremiah's chest. His breathing was heavy, labored. He was slipping away. I spoke under my breath, whispering as I called upon the elements one final time.

"Terra. Air. Ignis. Aqua. Spiritus. Sanabit. Sanabit. Sanabit!"

The Power flowed through me, using my shell as a vessel, and entered Jeremiah. As it passed, it refueled his strength, and within seconds, his eyelids fluttered open. I smiled as I pulled him to me, wrapping my arms around his strong frame.

"I thought you were a goner," I said in a chuckle.

"Me too," he replied.

I sat back and placed a kiss on his forehead. He smiled, and I wiped away the lipstick I'd left behind. I ignored the vampires who stared in disbelief. Instead, I scanned the room for Amicia, who stood on the stairs, surrounded by her personal guards. She smiled at me and nodded. I thought back to our conversation earlier today. She was right. Everyone would be watching, and now, no one would question where my loyalties lay.

CHAPTER
TEN

"THE ROGUES WILL return," I said, pacing Amicia's office as the other Hunters stood with arms crossed. Amicia said nothing as she tapped her nails against the top of her desk. "We need help."

"They *won't* help us, Avah. You know this," Jasik said.

"I have to try. If not, then what? What will we do? Wait for them to return? Try to fight? Jeremiah almost died!"

"But I didn't die. We can just harvest your witchy power or something, right? We can figure out a plan without your old coven's help," Jeremiah said.

"We can't harvest The Power. It doesn't work that way. I could fight a few at a time, but an army? I would need to fully embrace it. Tapping into that much of The Power would consume me. We need answers. I know the elders have information," I said, running a hand through my hair. "There has to be something in the prophecies that we can use."

"She's right," Amicia said. She raised a hand as Jasik began to speak. "Enough. This is not a discussion. I'm sending Avah to Shasta. The witches will give her guidance, and she'll return before sunrise the same eve. The Hunters will stay here to watch the manor."

"Milady, please," Jasik said.

"I have made my decision," she said as she stood. "I will not discuss this further. She is going. You will stay here to protect this coven. Avah, you leave at sundown, and you will return by sunrise. Is that clear?"

"Yes, Milady."

"No!" Jasik stopped pacing the room. "She's not going, Amicia. We need to find a way to contact the witches without sending Avah to her death."

"How *dare* you speak to me with such disrespect! Have you forgotten the price for such actions? Or are you simply blinded by this *ridiculous* love affair?" Amicia walked toward Jasik. Anger practically beamed from her.

"Wait!" I said, stepping between them, putting my arms up in surrender. "There *is* a way for me to contact my mother. We're both spirit users. We've both perfected our ability to astral project. I can go to her *tonight* without ever leaving your side," I said, turning toward Jasik.

I decided to not mention that astral projection would only work if my mother was willing. She was much more advanced and had the ability to block her mind from others. I knew mentioning that fact would force me on the road—and I wasn't prepared for the price Jasik's anger would cause him to pay.

"You can do this tonight?" Amicia asked.

"Yes. I can reach out to her mind while I sleep."

"Then it is done. Everyone to your chambers. Tomorrow, we prepare for war—with, I hope, help from the witches."

I left her office in a daze. The vampires of the house continued with their night. They had no idea. They didn't know of the danger that lurked. Amicia had assured them that my power had eliminated the threat. But in reality, I had only killed a few. Those who didn't perish ran.

I reached my door, closing it behind me and peeling

203

off my clothes. I turned on the shower and sat on the cold ground as the hot water cascaded over me. The steam rose, fogging the glass enclosure. I brought my legs up, covering my chest, and rested my head on my knees.

I thought about the fight to come and the likely event we'd die, I'd be taken, or The Power would consume me. I shuddered at the thought.

"Stop being so negative," I whispered, pulling my legs closer to me.

The door to the shower opened. Jasik stood before me with a look of defeat. He couldn't stop me from projecting to the witches—or traveling on foot if needed. He couldn't change how important I was to this coven. As much as he wanted to protect me, he couldn't. The toll weighed heavily on him even as he watched me.

"I'll be okay," I said, rubbing my arms up and down my legs. "We'll be okay."

"I just," he said, looking at the ground, "I couldn't bear it if anything were to happen to you. You've become part of me. I wouldn't survive it if they got to you before you made it to me." His tone was vulnerable, shaken.

"Jasik—"

He shook his head, silencing me. "Rest well tonight. You will need your strength for tomorrow." He turned to leave.

"Jasik, wait," I said, and he turned back to me.

I couldn't help stopping him. I couldn't stop what I'd subconsciously decided to do.

I stood. His eyes lingered on my nude body as I walked toward him. I scrunched his short hair beneath my fingers and pulled him down to meet my lips. He kissed me back with a ferocity I hadn't expected. He pushed me into the shower until I leaned against the wall. My fingers tore at his clothes, now wet from the shower, until we both stood nude. I jumped into his arms, my legs wrapping around his torso, and dug my fingers against his skin as he kissed my neck.

"Drink," I whispered, and he pulled back. I needed to feel that erotic bliss again.

"Soon, my love." He planted a trail of kisses down the length of my collar bone before his lips found mine again. "Tonight, there is no war. There is only you; there is only me."

He grabbed my thighs and slowly slid himself into

me. I moaned as he filled my body. He pumped faster, harder, and I dug my nails into his back, a trail of crimson dripping down the muscular curves. The smell of his blood and the intense pleasure of him inside me were almost too much.

He groaned as my nails broke skin, and in retaliation, he brought his lips to my neck and slowly lowered his fangs until they pierced my skin. He sucked long, hard, as he pumped faster.

I was acutely aware of the rough feeling of him rubbing inside of me, of his lips on my neck, of his tongue rubbing against the puncture marks to keep the wound open, of the force behind each suckle, of the water splashing against us, and of the growing sensation within me—one that would soon overpower my ability to hold it down.

I moaned as it overtook me and bit into Jasik's neck. I felt his essence splash into me as we both drank from each other. He pulled away breathlessly.

We stood in the shower, holding each other as the water slid down the curves of our bodies.

My chest rose and fell in quick bursts as I allowed my sputtering heart to slow. I rested my head against him as he wrapped his arms around me, running his fingertips down my spine. I shivered.

I gazed up at him and wrapped my arms around his neck, and for a brief moment, I felt safe, at peace.

I CLOSED MY eyes and focused on my mother, on her essence. I fought to ignore the overwhelming sensation to reach for Jasik, who lay nude beside me, with only a thin sheet separating him from me. I shivered at the thought of having him touch me again.

I exhaled deeply, focusing.

Breathe in through your nose and out through your mouth.

My breathing became heavier. Slowly, it became nonexistent. I let go of the human tendencies, the instinctual habits, as my astral self left its binding shell. Soon, I was hovering over my old house, terrified to enter.

Instead, I opted for the front door. We needed their help, and I couldn't afford to burn bridges.

I floated to the ground, looking around at the outside

world. I could see nothing beyond the fog. My legs were heavy as I walked to the door. Slowly, I balled my fist and knocked. I could only lift my arm three times before the weight of my limb overcame me, and it fell limp to my side.

I knew my mother was rejecting me. That was the only reason staying felt physically draining to an astral being. She didn't want to answer my call, but I couldn't afford to leave without her help.

"I know you can hear me. I know you know I'm here. Please, Mom. We need you. I need you." My words were barely above a whisper. It hurt to speak.

My breathing slowed, my body weak. I knew I couldn't hold on much longer without her.

"I won't leave. Not without speaking to you," I said.

The door creaked open. The silhouette of a person stood in the distance. Her back was to me. She was fiddling with a vase of white roses on the table. Even though I didn't recognize her, couldn't see her face, I knew it was my mother.

I took a step forward, attempting to enter the house, but I was stopped. With my hand before me, I touched the clear barrier that prevented me from entering my coven's home. I tried to push against it, silently begging for entrance. It did not give way.

"Why can't I enter?"

"Your kind is not welcome here," she said. She didn't turn toward me. She didn't look up when she spoke. She simply arranged the flowers. As she moved each rose, petals fell from the buds, drying and turning to dust as they hit the floor.

I tried to push my way into the house. I clenched my fist, brought my arm back, and banged on the barrier. I knocked again, over and over. It took what little strength I had left to not fall, to not return to my shell.

Her head jerked up, and the vase of dead roses fell from her hands, crashing to the ground and shattering into pieces. I blinked, and she disappeared. I blinked again, and she reappeared before me.

"Stop!" she yelled. "Do you really think the power of one vampire can withstand the power of an entire coven? You cannot break our barriers. Now you must leave here!"

"We need your help. Rogues, they're coming. They're coming for me."

"Avah, you know we can't help you anymore. You

need to figure this out on your own. Now please leave." She paused briefly before adding, "And don't come back."

A single tear slid down her cheek, but she turned away. When she faced me again, the tear was gone—replaced by the cold, hard stare with which she had welcomed me.

"I won't leave. Not until I can speak to the elders. I need to learn about The Power. I think it can help us."

She laughed. It was abrupt, mean. She stopped herself quickly. "You can't possibly believe that The Power is still within you. You died, Avah. The Power moves on to the next chosen one. You know the prophecy."

"No, it doesn't. I've used it. It's still within me." I tried to reassure her, but I was losing focus. If she didn't accept my astral self soon, I'd lose my connection to her.

"That's not possible..." she said, confused. She turned away from me, lost in her own thoughts.

"I'm still the same. Becoming a vampire didn't damn my soul. There's so much we didn't know—"

"Avah, stop! I can't help you. Not anymore. You must leave here."

"Not until I speak with the elders. They must know something. Rogues are coming, Mom. Whether you like it or not." I was angry, and I was sure it showed. I wouldn't budge. I'd die before I'd leave without information. I was stubborn, but I was my mother's daughter.

She sighed, and the barrier lifted. With her acceptance, I was rejuvenated. I felt life flow through me just as it had when I first left to meet her. I stood tall, strong. I inhaled deeply. The feeling of power within me washed over my insecurities, my fears. I smiled and stepped inside.

"You can't come back here, Avah. They won't let me help you. Things... things have changed since you've left. There are new people in power, and they won't let me help you." She ran her hand through my hair, tucking loose strands behind my ear.

"I don't understand. Are you not the high priestess anymore?"

"They may be listening. You must go!" Tears pooled in her eyes and threatened to spill.

"But we need help!"

"There's nothing I can do to help you anymore. You

must look within yourself." She placed her hand over my heart and closed her eyes.

Listen, Avah. Listen to your heart. Find the strength within.

"It's time to go back now. You've stayed too long."

I knew she was right. My astral self had been away from its shell far too long. I never knew what would happen if I stayed in The Beyond longer than necessary, and I didn't want to find out. I feared so much: The Power, Rogues, The Beyond... There was so much I didn't know or understand.

"But I still haven't any answers. I don't know how to use The Power."

She began pulling away. The world hazed over again, and through the smoke, I couldn't see her silhouette any longer.

"No! Not yet! I need to speak with the elders!"

I was hovering over my body. I watched as Jasik lay beside me, whispering into my ear. He told me to be strong, to find my way back to him. Briefly, I wondered how long I had been gone. It seemed like only mere seconds had passed.

My eyes fluttered open as I reentered my body. Jasik leaned over me, running his fingers across my cheek. He smiled at me and kissed my forehead.

I smiled back and wondered how I'd break the news: the witches weren't coming.

JASIK AND I dressed in silence. The words from our late night conversation echoed in my mind.

They won't help us.

I still couldn't believe it. I couldn't believe my own flesh and blood would leave us to die. I had accepted my new life as a vampire and the good I could accomplish with my newfound strength and immortality. Why couldn't they? I had the ability to avenge our coven. Why couldn't they see that? Why couldn't they see how useful I could be?

"So what happens now?" I asked, picking up where the conversation ended the night before.

"Today, we train in combat. We all must be prepared."

"What aren't you telling me?" I asked. Jasik and I hadn't known each other for long, but I could read him easily. The way he fidgeted; the way he avoided contact. He wanted something from me, something that could be dangerous, and he didn't know how to ask.

He exhaled dramatically and turned to face me. "We're also going to need something from you. The witches with whom we've aligned ourselves are unable to assist. Our magical defenses are weak. We need to strengthen the spells cast to protect us."

The thought of practicing magic again gave me butterflies. "Will that keep the Rogues from fighting?" I asked, hopeful.

"No, but it will provide us with necessary time."

I said nothing. Instead, I thought. I had cast protection and barrier spells countless times, but not since I'd become a vampire. The thought of tapping into my ancestral heritage excited me, but briefly, I wondered if I could still do it. I shook my head to wipe away the ridiculous thought. I could tap into The Power, so I could certainly tap into the magic I was born with.

"I'll do it."

THE HOUSE WAS eerily quiet as we made our way to breakfast. Very few vampires lingered in the hallways and dining hall.

"Where is everyone?" I asked between slurps. I had been surprised by how quickly I had become used to the taste of blood. I found it delicious and gave into my daily cravings. I relished in the thought of getting up to feed. I had quickly dismissed any thought of disgust, of fear. Feeding was a necessity now, and I was okay with that.

"Amicia has ordered everyone to stay in their chambers so that we may complete our tasks uninterrupted," he answered before taking the final gulp of his drink.

I nodded, threw my head back, and did the same. Before swallowing, I swished it around in my mouth, letting the warm liquid roll over my tongue. In a quick, unwanted burst, memories of my childhood flashed before my eyes.

I saw my six-year-old self sitting at our table. It was Yule morning. I was walking my Gingerbread cookies around the tabletop, on which I had arranged various condiment bottles. Each represented a different place:

my house, the supermarket, town square, and so on.

Suddenly, years flew by in a daze. I was ten, and I was attempting to build a cottage out of my waffles, failing miserably. Frustration got the best of me, and I tossed my plate of broken waffles into the garbage.

And then I was fifteen. I scraped my fork across the table, rolling my eyes as my cousins bickered in the corner. My mother chastised me for yet again playing with my food.

"What do you think, Avah?" Jasik asked, breaking me away from my thought. I swallowed hard.

"About what?"

"Today's itinerary."

"Oh, um… what's the plan again?"

"Are you feeling well?" Jasik asked, resting his hand atop mine.

"Yeah, sorry," I said, squeezing his hand. "Just thinking. What's today's plan, then?"

"The first thing we must do is strengthen the magic barriers. I'll leave you to that while I update Amicia on your visit last night. Afterward, we'll train. You'll need to learn control if we're to battle Rogues."

"Sounds good," I said while standing.

As we made our way out of the dining hall, I noticed that the few vampires lounging around took the time to stop and smile at me. I hadn't had much interaction with my housemates since the Rogue encounter, and though I knew my decision to protect the coven would create some relationship changes, I was still surprised to see how quickly I was accepted into their house. It was finally beginning to feel like home.

The basement quarters had an occult storage room that was stockpiled with herbs, crystals, and various ritual relics. Everything I needed to strengthen the original protection barriers was in the basement, and I found it strange that vampires had this much access to so many items used in witchcraft. These items were thought to be sacred, untouchable by immortals. As I ran my fingertips down the smooth edge of a pentacle, I realized even more so that so much I had been taught was wrong. I wasn't sure what was fact and what was fiction. It made me queasy to think that everything I had learned had been based on lies.

"Everything you should need is in this room," Jasik said.

"Yes, right. I guess I'll get started. I won't need long.

I'll just go through your stock, grab what I need, and meet you out front. The spell itself will take maybe a minute. All I can really do is add power to the original spell. Maybe try casting one of my own."

"Anything will help," he said with a smile.

I listened to his footsteps fade away as he walked down the hall and up the stairs. I exhaled deeply when I knew he was gone—and out of earshot.

"Okay, Avah. You can do this."

The small room had floor-to-ceiling shelving. In the center of the room was a large prep table. I grabbed a small cardboard box that was tossed in the corner and began tossing items into it: salt; iron shavings; silver pebbles; four quartz crystals; and powdered garlic, saffron, thyme, rosemary, sage, henbane, and aconite.

I laid the ingredients out on the table, pushing the quartz crystals to the side. I pulled a dust-ridden cauldron from the corner to the center of the room. I wiped it clean and dumped the ingredients into the pot.

I lit a bundle of sage and blew out the flame. The dried herb smoked, cleansing the room, as I grabbed an athamé. I waved the athamé through the cloud of smoke, cleansing the tool. Quickly tossing the sage to the side, I mixed the cauldron's contents with the tip of the athamé. Closing my eyes, I envisioned The Power, the protection the mixing would produce.

"Te invoco, Hecate, ariolatus est et observavit auguria deam. Venite ad me, et protector meus, in exsilium agere negativity, lucrum inde. Gun potestas mea. Custodi me, fiat!" I said, invoking the gods to purify and strengthen the contents so that we may use it for protection.

A warm mist clouded my senses as the elements obeyed my command, empowering the potion I had just created. I let out a squeal and opened my eyes. I had done it. I had called upon my magic, my Pagan heritage, and it obeyed.

I turned toward the table, leaving the cauldron where it sat, and focused on cleansing the quartz crystals as I waved the smoking sage over them. Cleansing had always been the easiest part of witchcraft. A little sage and good intentions went a long way.

With my ingredients finished, I grabbed the cauldron and crystals and went outside. The air was still, the world motionless. I imagined they watched me now. I ignored the overwhelming sensation to lower my fangs and growl at the night.

I gently took the quartz crystals out of the pot and set them on the porch. I walked to the edge of the property, stepping outside the gate. I closed my eyes, focusing on the power I had within me. In a quick motion, I ran around the perimeter of our property, dragging my feet as I went. Within minutes, I had run around a dozen times, and with each lap, I dug my heels into the ground. The groove provided ample room to bury my protection potion. In one final lap, I poured the potion into the dirt, burying it as I moved on.

"Dique deaeque omnes, ut sint propter te. Adjutorio domus. Protégé," I said as I moved around the house. Asking the gods and vampire goddess to protect us with this offering was easy. Knowing if they'd agree to protect a house of vampires was another issue altogether.

When the potion had been poured, I dropped the cauldron onto the porch and grabbed the quartz crystals. Quickly, I set one stone at each corner of the house— north, east, south, and west.

"Custodes speculis aquilonis clamavi ad te. Speculis tutores orientis clamavi ad te. Custodes speculis austri clamavi ad te. Custodes speculis occidentis clamavi ad te. Custodes speculis, quaeso te domum hanc!" I said, begging the guardians to protect

the beings of this house. My magic flowed freely into the crystals, sparking an inner glow. The light dimmed but remained lit. My spell had worked.

Smiling, I grabbed the cauldron and slowly walked up the steps of the manor. I twisted the doorknob and pulled the creaking door open, and then I heard it: a twig breaking in the distance, the rumble of feet pounding against the hard-packed ground, and the low growl of Rogues in the distance. I turned back, listening. They grew quiet. The spell was still strong. It would hold until daybreak. I was sure of it.

I didn't know who was out there. I didn't know why they wanted me. But I did know one thing...

"Tomorrow, we end this."

CHAPTER
ELEVEN

THE PALM OF his hand found the center of my chest in a quick jab. I was propelled backward. I hit the brick wall with a force that pushed the air out of my lungs. Chunks of brick fell beside me, a cloud of dust coating the air. I pushed myself off the ground, the bones in my chest slowly healing from the brush of death.

As I stood, my fangs lowered, and I instinctively took a predatory stance.

"Good, but you need to learn to counter attack, Avah," Jasik said. I brushed off my hands and rolled my eyes.

"Yeah, yeah. I know." My fangs retracted, and I kicked the pieces of stone by my feet.

"This is important. They want you, and they will stop

at nothing to get you."

"Thanks for reminding me. There's a Big Bad out there, and it only wants to play with me." I crossed my arms over my chest. I pretended I wasn't worried, but it was all a lie. I knew Jasik could sense my growing nervousness, but I still tried to hide it. I needed everyone to believe I was as strong as they seemed to think I was.

Jasik eliminated the space between us. He placed his fingertips under my chin and lifted my head to meet his gaze.

"I'll stop at nothing to protect you," he whispered. The words rolled off his tongue, coated in the sweet English accent I longed to hear.

I smiled up at him and pulled him into a long, passionate kiss. We pulled away breathlessly.

"Well, look at the two lovebirds," Lillie said, walking into the training quarters.

I stepped away from Jasik, wiping away any evidence that his lips met mine.

"No need to stop on my account," she said, rolling her eyes.

Malik and Jeremiah followed behind her. Malik's seriousness often matched Jasik's, but Jeremiah could always be spotted with a cheeky grin plastered on his face. I nudged him in the gut as he passed me. He dramatically clutched his side and howled in pain. I bit back laughter.

"So what's the plan, Boss?" Jeremiah asked, grabbing a dagger and twirling it in his hand.

"We already know how to fight together. I'm more worried about Avah. She still hasn't tapped into all of her abilities."

"We can reenact the fun brawl in the woods," he said. He smiled and winked at me.

"And risk her nearly killing you again? I think not," Lillie said. She grabbed the dagger from Jeremiah's hand, spun it around, and tossed it through the air. It flew by my face with precision accuracy. As it whipped through the air, only centimeters from slicing my cheek, it seemed to move in slow motion. I reached forward, grabbing the weapon by the tip of the blade and threw it back—only I didn't miss. The thin blade planted itself in the center of a bull's eye poster that was pinned to the wall behind Lillie.

"Nice!" Jeremiah said, annunciating each syllable of the word.

"She seems to be well-trained," Malik said.

"I was a hunter at one point, too," I said, remembering my days of hunting vampires on our property. I realized too late that that was probably not the best thing to say in a room full of vampires.

"Your past training will be a great asset," Jasik said. His words were comforting.

"I think so. I've trained for years. I'm ready for this." I hoped my enthusiasm would give them more confidence in me, because even though they joked and smiled and played, I knew they wondered if I was ready for this fight. But what they didn't realize was that I had been preparing for this fight my entire life.

"You can train her for centuries, Jasik, but you and I both know that won't matter," Malik said. He and Jasik shared a knowing glance.

"What does that mean?" I asked.

"It means you'll never learn to truly control your abilities until you're forced to use them."

"So, you're saying—"

"He's saying there's no better time or place to learn to use your gift than in the midst of a war," Jasik said.

I said nothing. I knew he was right. Emotion

controlled my abilities. The only time I'd used them was when I was angry or scared. Not once was I in a controlled environment simply begging them to come out.

"Basically just throw me in the game and hope I make it out alive?" I asked. It sounded harsher than I meant it to be, and the pain of my words danced across Jasik's face.

"Malik is right. There's no point in trying to force a reaction. Your abilities will come out naturally. And there's no need to train you to fight when you were born to be a Hunter," Jasik said.

Born to be a Hunter. I had never thought of it that way, but there had been few things in life I'd excelled at—and being a Hunter was one of them.

"So then what's the plan?" I asked.

"While you were casting protection spells, we contacted the local covens. They can't afford to send aid. Not when this many Rogues are so close to home. With Hunters protecting their own covens, we'll be alone in this battle."

"Wait. What about the witches?" Lillie asked.

"The witches... They're unavail—"

"They're not coming," I interrupted. "We're on our own."

"Ouch. I bet that hurt," she replied.

It did, but I couldn't think about that now. We needed a plan. We needed to figure out a way to protect this house and everyone in it without any casualties, and that wasn't so hard, right?

"About the spell… Without having something to tie the spell to, it'll only hold its strength until daybreak. After that, it'll begin weakening," I said.

"Daybreak? That's it? That's all the time we have?" Lillie asked, pacing the floor. "You know, this is all your fault," she said, pointing at Jasik. "You just couldn't let her die—"

"Lillie—" Malik cut in.

"Why would you say that?" Jeremiah said.

"Enough!" Jasik said. "This stops, Lillie. Now! Nothing you say will change the past. Let it go, or I'll find another resolution."

Lillie gasped. "You wouldn't!"

"We can't work like this, and you know that. You're angry at me. I understand that. I broke the law. I understand that, as well. But I will not be reminded of your hatred of Avah day after day. There will be more suitable covens for you to protect, if it comes to that."

I was baffled. Lillie had been with this coven for years, yet he would send her away. He would trade her... for me. I didn't know why I found that surprising. We were pretty much dating, but it still felt wrong. I didn't want to be *that* girl: the one who got in the way, the one who destroyed relationships.

"Stop this! We have bigger, more serious, deadlier problems!" I said. I turned to Lillie. "You hate me. I get that. I still don't care, so get over it!" I turned to Jasik. "And you. You're not sending her away, because this isn't going to happen again. No one in this room can change the past, so it's time to get over it. I'm here, and I'm not leaving. Now can we *please* talk about the army of Rogues that are waiting outside our door?"

"She's right. I'm sorry," Lillie said, and for once, I believed her.

"Great, now as I was saying, the spell will only keep its strength until daybreak; then it'll slowly start to lose power."

"Why is that?" Jeremiah asked. "I mean, we've had spells protecting us for years. Why did they last so long?"

"They had an entire coven cast them, and they probably were tied to something. There's nothing happening right now to tie the spell to."

"Like what?"

"Like a full moon, a lunar eclipse, something. Believe it or not, there is more to a *strong* spell than simply tossing some herbs on the ground and saying some words."

"All right. Worst case scenario: the spell weakens enough for Rogues to pass through. That happens at daybreak, but the sun will provide protection until sunset. That's when they'll come."

"I think now's a good time to talk about evacuation," I said.

"Avah, they'll never stop looking for you. You have eternity to run, but so do they."

"No, not for me. For them," I said, signaling to the house. "For the vampires here. We should get them out of here."

Yes," Jasik said, rubbing his chin. "That could work." He seemed lost in thought.

"Or we could talk about a possibly really good plan that will very likely work, but I'm pretty positive you're going to hate it," I said.

The vampires stared back at me, curiosity in their eyes.

I swallowed hard and explained my plan.

CHAPTER
TWELVE

I CLOSED MY eyes as the water cascaded down. I had woken before the alarm alerted me that it was three in the afternoon. I hadn't been up this early since I had transitioned. The sun would soon set, and though I always welcomed night, today, I feared it. I knew my vampire housemates felt the same terror as they hurried down the halls, preparing for, what I could only assume to be, the battle of our lifetime.

We had stayed awake well into the morning hours, devising our plan, informing Amicia that we had no other choice. The Rogues were coming, and we couldn't stop them. We couldn't run from them. All we could do was fight.

Jasik immediately disapproved of my plan. I hadn't

assumed anything less when I laid it all out for them. Though, I hadn't expected the others to side with me—especially not Malik, Jasik's overly loyal brother. An even bigger shock came from support from Lillie.

I rubbed the back of my neck between my hands, massaging away the kinks that had formed overnight. Closing my eyes, I took several deep breaths. I was exhausted—mentally and physically. The magic I had used earlier drained me, and I didn't have enough time to refuel. I hoped a few dozen blood bags after my shower would do the trick.

The bathroom door opened, and I heard Jasik's voice.

"Should I wait for you?"

"Yeah, I'm getting out now," I said.

We walked in silence into the dining hall. The empty halls were eerily quiet. There were no service providers, so we helped ourselves to the stock of blood in the walk-in refrigerator. Our supply seemed dangerously low. I assumed I wasn't the only vampire hoping blood would give me the strength I needed to survive the coming hours. Jasik and I drained a dozen bags each within minutes. I still felt hungry, and he urged me to drink more.

"You're weak from your spellcasting. You must refuel, Avah," he said.

"Our supply is dwindling. We'll need the rest for... for after." I looked at the ground, nervously picking at my nails. I didn't know why I was so scared. Something else was haunting me. In the pit of my stomach, something felt *wrong*. I knew Rogues were out there, probably closer than we realized, but something else had been nagging at me ever since I had told the Hunters of my plan.

It felt like something else was out there, watching, waiting, buying time. I couldn't shake the feeling.

"I'm okay. Really," I said, flashing a fake smile. "Let's just get ready." I closed the door to the refrigerator and walked toward the basement. I took the steps two at a time and walked into the training quarters. The other Hunters were already there, busily strapping on weapons.

We all dressed identically. I supposed it marked us as Hunters. Though we were scantily dressed, it didn't feel as such. When adorned with weapons, one couldn't help but feel powerful, strong, covered.

I could have worn anything, and I found it ironic that

I was drawn to wear the outfit I chose. I had begged Jasik to give me another option when he first tossed these clothes at me. Now, they felt empowering. While wearing this outfit, I faced my biggest threat: me.

"Let me help you with this," Jasik said, holding the scabbard. I slipped my arms through. It fit snugly, tighter than before. I wondered if Jasik made alterations after my last... encounter with it.

"Thanks," I said, smiling.

I opened the cabinet containing various scabbards and strap-on sheaths, pulling several out. I slipped one onto each leg, tightening the straps so they fit snugly around my thighs. The black fabric seemed to disappear against my spandex shorts.

I slid an ankle sheath over my black tennis shoes and secured a small blade. I grabbed two daggers and put them into my hip sheaths. Briefly, I wondered if I was overdoing it. I glanced at Lillie, who had just finished strapping a katana on her back. She looked up as I counted her blades, and when our eyes met, we shared a small, knowing smile.

The katana on her back glistened in the light, and I found myself missing my old weapon. It had broken in the vampire fight, and I hadn't had time to get it repaired before I changed. I knew I'd never see it again, and I found that oddly discomforting.

I shook the feeling away by walking to the wall of weapons. My baby sat there. Clean, untouched since it last violated me and my trust. I imagined Jasik spending countless hours cleaning it down here while I slept. The thought made me smile.

I grasped the handle of the seax with my hand and pulled it from its spot on the wall. I took a few steps to the side so I could watch myself in the wall of mirrors.

This was it. This was my test.

I closed my eyes and twirled the blade in my hand, focusing on the grooves of the handle and how they skidded across the sensitive skin on my palm. My body moved as twirled the weapon, my hair whipping around as I spun. It moved beautifully with me. The blade matched my rhythmic thrusts, twists, and turns, and as I spun the weapon up and brought it down toward me, it slid into its sheath. My arm fell to my side, and I opened my eyes. The other vampires were watching me, and as they nodded in approval, Jasik simply smiled. In that moment, I knew everything would be okay. I knew the

Rogues were out there, I knew we would soon go into battle, but most importantly, I knew we would win.

We walked upstairs in silence. Silence was something I was beginning to get used to while living in this house. There never seemed to be the right words.

The vampires of the house were piled in the foyer, waiting for their next command. Amicia stood at the top of the stairs, her guards on each side of her. The floor cleared as we walked into the room, the vampires parting like the Red Sea. They looked nervous, frightened.

The Hunters and I made our way to the front door and turned around to face them. I didn't know what to say, and I wasn't sure anyone else did either. I licked my lips and cleared my throat. All eyes fell to me.

"I know you're all scared," I began, unsure of what to say next. I looked up at Jasik, hands shaking. Sure, public speaking wasn't my forte, but this was getting pathetic. How was I to lead them into battle when I didn't even have the strength to make a simple speech? Jasik grabbed onto my hand, sliding his fingers between mine, and squeezed. He smiled at me and nodded, urging me to go on. We didn't have much time now. The sun was already setting.

"I know you're all scared, and honestly, I was, too. When I came here, I was terrified. Everything I thought I knew had been taken from me. My world shattered in a matter of minutes. And then I came here, and I met all of you. I was still scared, but at some point," I looked at the ground, shaking my head, "and I don't even know when," I looked up, meeting the gaze of a small blonde who looked no older than fifteen, "my fear was replaced with something I had longed for. I finally found my place here, with all of you. I don't understand much about being a vampire, and I don't know why I'm here, why I survived the change, or why I'm different, but I do know one thing…"

I paused. I lowered my jaw as my fangs lowered. I tapped into The Power within me and felt it radiate off me in waves. The vampires surrounding me gasped and stepped backward.

"No one threatens my family and lives." There was an anger, a power, a ferocity to my voice—one I had never heard. I threw my head back and bellowed. My arms out beside me, I pulled at The Power nestled deep within me. The Power was strong and yielding. As it blasted from me, the house shook from roof to foundation.

I heard the rumble of footsteps outside. The Rogues were coming for us. My display of power wasn't enough to make them change their minds—a mistake they'd only make once.

I met the gazes of the other Hunters. With glowing irises that seemed to burn into mine, with elongated fangs and hands clutching blades, they were ready to fight—and die—for this coven, just as I was.

I turned back to Amicia's guards and said, "Keep her safe." They nodded, clutched her arm, and began pulling her toward the basement.

When she reached the bottom of the stairs, she grabbed onto my hand and said, "It has been an honor knowing you, Avah. You will make one hell of a leader some day." She smiled, and then she was gone, her vampire guards following closely behind her as they escorted her to safety. I had learned of the hidden rooms in the basement long before we needed an escape plan. The secret tunnels were only an added benefit.

"Take your places," I said, and the vampires broke into groups, leaving the foyer.

The Hunters before me took a step back, lining up.

In unison, they lifted their right hands and placed them across their chests, their clutched fists resting against their hearts. I didn't fully understand the meaning behind the action, but I was honored they had bestowed it upon me. I mirrored their actions before turning to walk out the front door.

"Avah," Jasik said, grasping my wrist and pulling me to him. I fell against him, our lips meeting as if that were their natural resting place. His hand clutched the back of my neck, pushing me harder against him. The embrace was passionate but short-lived, because almost as soon as it began, he pulled away and whispered, "Be careful."

I nodded and walked out the front door. The Hunters followed suit. I didn't look back until I reached the gate that surrounded our property. The gate served as the spell's barrier, and once we stepped beyond its borders, we were no longer protected by my magic. I looked behind me and to my right, where Jasik stood. Jeremiah stood behind him and to his right. I looked behind me and to my left, where Malik stood. Lillie stood behind him and to his right.

The Rogues approached, standing only yards from the gate's door. I faced them. They walked with a sly arrogance, like they knew they'd win this war. I smiled on the inside, because I knew they were wrong.

"You're even more beautiful than I remembered," a man said as he stepped forward. I remembered him from the night they attacked the ball. Sticks cracked underfoot. Briefly, he was distracted.

"Did you just come here to talk? Because I've heard it all before," I said, hoping to divert his curiosity from the world behind us.

He laughed loudly, gripping his stomach in a dramatic showcase. I rolled my eyes.

"My offer still stands. Your life for their lives. It only seems fair." He flashed a wide smile. He was confident I'd give up my life for my family. In a way, he was right. I would die for them, but I'd take the Rogues with me.

"You know that's not going to happen," I said.

"I thought you might say that," he replied, and with the snap of his fingertips, his army of Rogues fled from the shadows and raced toward our gate.

I reached back, yanked my seax from its sheath, and twirled the weapon in the palm of my hand.

"Leave him for me," I ordered, and in a dash, we left the safety of the barrier to end this.

CHAPTER
THIRTEEN

I WATCHED JEREMIAH'S shield go up around the manor as an added extra precaution. The night we planned today's defense, he had told me he'd die before he'd let his shield fall. I only hoped that would never be the case.

I brought my blade down on a Rogue, slicing through his neck. His head fell to the ground beside his body. I brought my blade up again, slicing through another's torso. He fell to the ground. They surrounded us. It was five against what seemed to be a hundred. Their numbers rolled down the hills toward us, with no end in sight.

I fought my way toward the leader, killing Rogues as I passed. The first step in hunting was to determine the leader. The next step was to eliminate that threat. As I made my way toward him, my mind began to clear. I focused on only him—and the thought of my blade slicing open his neck.

I skidded to a stop as two Rogues hauled toward me. With the flick of my wrist, I sheathed my seax and quickly took my two daggers in hand. When they were only feet before me, I jumped into a high backflip. They passed below me but not before my daggers slid into their eye sockets. I landed on my feet, pulling my seax and slicing it forward. They dropped to their knees, dead. I re-sheathed my daggers and scoured the ground for the leader. I knew he couldn't be far. As more Rogues approached, I knew I didn't have much time.

I scanned the crowd, sidestepping a Rogue. I twirled my seax and slid it behind me. She cried out and fell to her knees. I brought my arm back up, pulling the seax from her gut. She was dead before her limp body hit the ground. My eyes found Jasik. He and Malik were cornered. Malik's gift as a seer made it difficult to defeat him, but I could tell Jasik was relying on his ability to heal. Pain flashed across his face as the Rogues attacking him landed a hit.

Rogues were savage creatures. They relied on their hands and strength to fight, not weapons. Stupidly, I had thought weapons would be our advantage, but I couldn't imagine the power of their fists. From across the field, I heard Jasik's jaw break when a Rogue's fist landed its hit.

I reached his side in seconds, slamming my foot against the back of the Rogue's calf. He fell to the ground. I wrapped my arm around his head and twisted. His neck snapped, and I drove my blade into his skull. I killed the final Rogues that cornered him and dropped to Jasik's aid.

"Are you okay?" I said. In a quick twist, he realigned his jaw, and it began to heal.

He nodded and stood.

I quickly searched the ground. We had killed a few dozen Rogues, but we had barely made a dent in the number of our attackers. I brought my blade down, beheading a girl who stupidly jumped in front of me, and made eye contact with Lillie.

Lillie, plan B.

I couldn't call out. I couldn't elaborate. I could only hope she was reading my mind at that moment. I knew Jasik wouldn't listen. I couldn't go to him. He had hoped we could end this ourselves, but I was growing tired. I was weakening, and so were they. We needed to be realistic. We needed our coven. Calling upon them came with unavoidable consequences, because we knew they wouldn't all make it.

When I explained my plan to Jasik, he had told me there would be no way Amicia would agree to it, but as soon as I explained how my magic could help them, he was more hopeful. When we brought the plan to Amicia, we hadn't expected her immediate approval.

"We have a plan," I had said. "We're going to ask the vampires of this house to fight for it, but a piece of me will be with each of them. I'll bless their weapons and bind my power to each of them with runes. That will give them the strength they need to make the kills, and if they stay in groups, they should be fine. We shouldn't lose many."

"All right," she had said, and I was sure my jaw hit the floor.

"Really?" I had said. "You're okay with it?"

She explained that this was a time of war, and in a war, casualties were unavoidable. I had prepared a solid defense—one that I was certain I'd have to use. Instead,

I was sent away to do her magical bidding. Binding myself to their weapons was tricky. It would leave me vulnerable, but I was willing to risk my life for theirs.

Lillie killed the Rogue in front of her and then side-stepped another. She ran toward the gate and dove past the barrier. She jumped to her feet and turned back, blades ready. The Rogues who pursued her slammed into the barrier I had cast. She smiled, turned back toward the manor, and disappeared through the front door.

She was only gone for minutes before they all emerged. Every vampire in the house came to our aid. They wore loose-fitting clothes, clutched knives and swords that had been blessed with my magic, and screamed as they ran toward the group of Rogues impatiently awaiting them. I don't know how I found the time to smile at their efforts, but I did.

"Remember to stay with your groups!" I called out. "Don't separate—"

Something hit me from behind. My body fell limp as I flew through the air and slammed into a tree. My spine broke, and I fell to the ground. I began to heal, but the Rogues were already upon me. I wouldn't heal fast enough, so I did the only thing I could do: I once again relied on my Pagan ancestry to save me.

"*Terra, Air, Ignis, Aqua, Spiritus, I appeho. Sanabit. Sanabit. Sana me!*" I barely spoke above a whisper, but it was enough. The tingling effects of my magic swirled around my broken spine, strengthening its core as the vampire blood within me reformed bone.

A Rogue reached me before I had use of my limbs. He pulled me to my feet, holding me in the air by a hand around my neck. I choked on blood as he crushed bone beneath his grip.

Focus! You don't need the breath to live.

"You should have taken option A, my sweet," a voice said. I opened my eyes to find the Rogue leader before me, smiling, baring fangs.

"Avah!" Jasik yelled from across the field. I trailed my eyes across the wasteland of dead bodies and found him. He ran toward me, pushing past the Rogues that tried to stop him. I tried to reach out to him, but my spine hadn't fully healed. I could feel it snapping back into place, and though I couldn't speak, inside I screamed.

"Kill him," their leader said, waving his arm dismissively. The Rogue released me, and I fell into the leader's arms. My head rested against his neck. He lifted me slightly, allowing me a clear view of the chaos behind him. Jasik fought the Rogues around him, but his eyes never left mine.

"I have big plans for you and me, Avah. We're going to rule *everything*," he whispered.

My spine made one final crack, and with its alignment, I dug my nails into his scalp, yanked his head back, and tore through his neck. I viciously drained him until his skin sunk into bone. I tossed him aside and moved my head from side to side, cracking the joints.

I released a deafening growl, and the Rogues froze. Their eyes went from me to their dead leader and back to me again. I growled as they screamed for their lost brother. They dropped their victims where they stood and charged me. With the help of the vampires, the Rogues' numbers were dwindling, but there were still a few dozen left.

I threw my hands to the sky and yelled, "*Incendia!*" I brought my hands back down as sparks flew from my fingertips. The Rogues combusted before me, and as more pursued me, the fire began to spread. I fell to my knees as my power drained my strength, but I refused to release the spell. I held on until I collapsed onto my side. As the final Rogues reached me, I found myself counting: one, two, three… Thirteen Rogues remained. I tried to laugh at the irony but fell short.

I smiled at Jasik, who was yelling my name and running to my aid. I knew he'd never reach me in time, but I wasn't upset. I'd leave this new world the way I came into it: fighting.

Just as the first Rogue reached my side, he turned to ash. Another turned to ash. Soon, they all were lit by a spark and fell to their deaths. I squeezed my eyes shut as I was lifted from the ground, a searing pain soaring through me. I needed to feed, and I needed to feed *now*. My eyelids were heavy, and it took everything I had to keep them open.

I opened my eyes when the pain subsided, and I found Jasik staring back at me, jaw clenched, machete in hand. The other Hunters matched his stance. Slowly, my eyes moved from Jasik, to Malik, to Jeremiah, to Lillie, and to the remaining vampires of our coven. Confused, I swallowed hard and rolled my head over. My breath caught.

The world around me seemed to disappear as I

stared at my savior. I ignored everything around me, because all I could see was a set of glowing violet irises staring back at me.

CHAPTER
FOURTEEN

BEEP. BEEP. BEEP. The machine blared at me. I swallowed; my mouth was dry, my tongue rough.

"H—Hello?" I said. I brought my hands to my eyes and peeled off the taped cotton pads. I opened my eyes but instantly shut them again. The light in the room was blinding. Slowly, I began to open them again, allowing my senses to adjust.

The room was illuminated by a dim bedside lamp. I looked around. I wore a hospital gown, and IVs of blood were taped to my arms. I sat up. I grunted as I moved off the cot.

"Hello?" I said again. "Jasik?"

The hall outside my room was dark. I pulled the needles from my veins and dropped them on the bed.

Blood dripped from the needles, soaking into the white cotton sheets. I stood and stumbled to the doorway. Pushing open the door, I entered the hallway and immediately recognized it as the basement quarters.

I leaned against the wall as I limped toward the stairs. I crawled up on my hands and knees. I didn't understand why I was so weak, but I didn't care. I needed to find Jasik and the others. I pulled myself into the foyer. I called out again, but no one answered. I pushed myself to my feet and fell against a small end table. The front door was open. I reached for it and wobbled onto the front porch.

And I saw them.

Jasik, Malik, Jeremiah, and Lillie were hanging from trees, their torsos split from navel to neck. Their innards were splattered on the ground, where the limbs of our coven mates lay dead. I screamed as I fell to the ground, clawing my way toward them.

"Now, now, Avah. You're not supposed to be awake yet," a voice said from behind. His accent was thick, Australian. "I hoped to clean this up a bit first," he said as a needle entered my throbbing neck.

The world grew dark as my eyes fluttered shut.

I WOKE SCREAMING and thrashing. Someone grabbed onto my arms, holding me down. I opened my eyes to find Jasik on top of me with fear-filled eyes.

I grabbed onto him and pulled him down to me. I wrapped my arms around his neck, burying my face into the crevice.

"I think... I think I just had a vision. It felt *so* real. You were dead. You were all dead," I said as tears spilled.

"It's okay. It's okay," he said, running his hand through my hair. "We're fine."

"No, you weren't. You were dead! I saw you! You—You—" I wasn't able to suck in as much air as I was letting out. I hiccupped and pulled him closer to me.

"Avah, look at me," he said, pulling away. He cupped my face between his palms, and I met his gaze. He smiled. "I'm okay. Malik, Lillie, and Jeremiah are all okay. We did it, Avah. *You* did it."

I wiped my tears away and pushed my lips against

his. I kissed him long and hard, unable to stop, to let him go. The dream had been so real. Images of him hanging flashed before my eyes, and I pulled away from him, shaking my head.

"I still see it. I see you hanging. You were cut open. Everyone was dead!" I said, running fingers through my matted hair.

"We did lose some. Maybe that's what you saw," he said, trying to reassure me.

"No, it was you." I nodded. "It was you. And it was real; it was *so* real. And there was... there was someone there. A man. He came from behind. He—he... he drugged me or something. I didn't see his face." I groaned in frustration.

"Do you remember anything from the fight?" he asked.

"What? No. I mean, I don't know. I just remember the man. I can't think of anything else but that stupid man and his thick accent. He talked to me. He told me I woke too soon. There were things he still needed to do," I said, looking up at Jasik.

"We have a visitor. A man. He's... like you."

Suddenly, I forgot all about my vision as scenes from

the fight flooded my mind. I remembered everything—especially *him*.

"Take me to him," I said.

"I will, but there are some things you need to know." His face grew somber as he recounted the facts I had missed while recovering.

Nearly forty-eight hours had passed.

We had lost seventeen vampires from our coven.

Amicia was missing. Her guards were dead.

I opened by mouth to speak but couldn't find words. I stood in a daze. How had so much time passed? How did we lose so many? Who had Amicia? *What happened?* Somehow, I knew our new visitor had information we needed. I knew he could help us locate Amicia, but I also wasn't sure he'd give up information willingly. Information meant leverage. I was sure there was something he wanted from us—or just from me.

"Has he said anything?" I asked as we took the stairs to Amicia's office.

"Only that he'll only speak with you."

"He isn't going to just give up what we need. If he has information, he'll likely want something in return. After all, it's pretty obvious we're desperate. We'll need to make him talk. There's no time for negotiations," I said.

"Are you sure you're ready for this?" Jasik asked as he grasped the doorknob to Amicia's office.

I nodded. My stomach growled, but I suppressed the need to feed.

The vampire was sitting at the chair beside Amicia's desk; the other Hunters watched him closely, ready to strike at any moment. I vaguely heard Jasik enter the office behind me and close the door. I was too focused on the vampire.

He was tall, thin, and had light, sandy brown hair that fell to just below his chin. His skin was pale, his eyes ice-cold, but what concerned me most were the violet irises that found me the moment I entered the room—and never looked away.

"Who are you?" I asked.

"Name's Sebastian, darlin', and I reckon you're Avah. Heard a lot about you," he said with a smile.

"H—How?" I asked, staring into his violet irises.

"How what? How'd I know your name, or how is there someone else like you out there?"

I didn't know what to say. I had so many questions.

There was so much I didn't understand, but I knew I needed to play my cards right. He had information I needed, and if he was smart, he'd use that to get something in return. I could only hope he was stupider than he looked.

"You see, darlin', there's a lot you don't know. There's a lot that coven of yours never told you 'bout this world. I reckon you've already figured that part out, though, eh?"

"What don't I know? How did you know about me? How did you *find* me?"

"Well," he said, standing from the chair and stretching, "that's a long story, and maybe if I wasn't so thirsty and received a little better hospitality, I could tell you all about it."

I furrowed my brows and stepped forward, angered.

"I want to make one thing very clear, Sebastian: We're not friends. I don't know you, and I don't owe you anything."

"Now wait just one minute! I *saved* all of you," he said, pointing to the other Hunters in the room. "And I think that—"

"Well, you thought wrong," I said, interrupting him.

"You're a testy one, eh?" he said with a smile.

"We don't have time for this. Just tell us what you know."

"I don't know anything about that priestess of yours. I reckon I got here *after* she was taken. 'Sides, I was a little busy *saving* all of you. Only stuck around 'cause I thought that might be worth something. Y'know, like *trust*."

"I don't even know you," I said. "I don't know that you weren't helping the Rogues in the first place. You both conveniently found me here."

"Blechh!" he said as he spat. "Rogues are foul creatures. I would never lower myself to having such tasteless friends."

"Say I believe you. Then what? What do you want? Why are you here?"

"Long story short: I'm here for you. In case you haven't noticed, we have just a few things in common."

"What do you want with me?" I felt my pulse racing. I wasn't sure if I wanted to know the answer.

He smiled, his gaze trailing down my frame. "Well, it's not too often a chosen one turns. Had to come see you for myself. Thought we could get to know each other, learn some things."

"Yeah? Like what?"

"I'm sure there are a few things you're dying to know. I turned a long while ago, but let's see if I can remember," he said, closing his eyes. "What am I? How'd this happen? Do I still have The Power? Am I still a witch? Will my coven ever welcome me back? What do I do now? Are there any more like me?" He opened his eyes. "Am I close?"

"Very," I said.

"Thought so."

"Is this just a guessing game, or do you plan to answer these burning questions sometime soon?"

"It'll take some time, but I'll oblige. I have a few conditions, of course."

"Of course," I said, rolling my eyes.

"First thing, the hospitality in this place sucks, and I want a room. A nice room. With a view."

"Oh, certainly. I mean, we wouldn't want our sun-stricken guest to miss a sunrise."

His mouth curved into a sideways smile. "There's so much you need to learn, Avah. I admire your innocence, your naivety. You'll soon lose both. Enjoy 'em while they last."

"The next condition?" Jasik asked.

"Avah and I speak alone," he said.

"Out of the question," Jasik said. "And the next condition?"

"Jas—" I said.

"There is no other condition—well, a supply of blood would be fantastic, too, but other than that, I require nothing else," Sebastian replied.

"You may believe Avah to be naïve, but I am wise beyond my years. Do you truly believe I would ever leave her alone with you?" Jasik asked.

"Do you *truly* believe I would tell her *anything* with you around?" Sebastian asked with a chuckle.

"You guys—" I said.

"You will not be left alone with her. End of discussion. Now, tell—"

"I really don't think it's up to you. Avah seems to be the leader of this pathetic excuse of a team," he said, his eyes glancing from Hunter to Hunter. "She can decide for her—"

"Stop!" I yelled, the earth shaking as power radiated from me. "We don't have time for this!"

"Now, now. No need to get fussy. If you think we don't have time for *this*, then you really don't want to bring about an earthquake," Sebastian said, crossing his arms.

"You'll get a room and some blood, but that's it."

"Then I tell you nothing, sweet pea."

"Excuse me?" I said. "I just agreed to two of your three conditions. That's a win for you. Take it or leave it," I said.

"Fine," he said. "Be seeing ya."

"You don't seem to understand, Sebastian. I'll keep you here. I'll wait until you're nice and weak, and then I'll walk right up to you and bite into that sweet Aussie neck of yours. I'll drink until you're begging me to stop, because you just can't take another minute of it." As I walked toward him, he took several steps back until he was pushed up against the wall. "Sooner or later, I'll get the answers I need from you. Or you can take the easy route and just tell me what I want to know."

His lips formed into the curve of a sideways grin. I was sure the smile plastered on his face was his go-to look. It probably melted the hearts of girls all across the globe, but to me, that grin spoke of an unknowable power—and of knowledge. In the end, I knew we'd pay for the knowledge he held over us, but right now, I couldn't think of that.

"You're feisty. I like that in a girl," he said, leaning forward. His nose touched mine, and his eyes fell to my lips.

I could practically hear Jasik tense from behind me as I took several steps back. Sebastian walked forward but stopped short of reaching me. Instead, he pulled a long-stem white rose from one of Amicia's vases. He brought his wrist to his mouth and tore through skin. Without averting his gaze, he dipped the tip of the flower into the wound. He slowly but confidently closed what little space separated us and held the blood rose just below my nose. A crimson line dripped down the curve of the delicate flower before collecting at the base and sliding down the stem. I met his eyes.

"Have a taste, then."

My fangs instinctively lowered, my tongue tracing the bottoms of my teeth. His gaze lowered, where he watched my tongue slide across my inner lip.

I didn't know what I'd feel once I tasted his blood, but I knew it wouldn't be anything good.

ACKNOWLEDGEMENTS

Writing is a team sport. I devoted a seemingly endless number of hours to writing this book, and I couldn't have done so without a select group of individuals. *Blood Rose* is dedicated to my team of friends and family who've helped me get this book to print, especially the following: my husband and my mom; my amazing editor, Tara from Narrative Ink Editing LLC; my graphic designer, Robin from Wicked by Design; and my undergraduate and graduate school mentors, Nancy Holder, David Anthony Durham, Theodora Goss, Dean Karpowicz, Carole Vopat, and Nick Tryling.

But most importantly, I want to thank my publisher, Oftomes Publishing. Thank you for giving me and my books a chance; I can't wait to take this writing journey with you.

WHAT HAPPENS IN THE NEXT BOOK?

READ ON FOR AN EXTRACT FROM

DANIELLE ROSE'S

BLOOD
MAGIC

OUT AUGUST 1st 2017

DANIELLE ROSE

"INTENSE AND INTRIGUING."
NEW YORK TIMES BESTSELLING AUTHOR, WENDY HIGGINS

BLOOD MAGIC

CHAPTER
ONE

AS A MORTAL witch destined to fight in a war against immortal vampires, my life had been surrounded by death. Before my birth rite, the ritual in which I obtained The Power, the ultimate weapon against the vampire race, I had even prepared for my own death. Being chosen came with consequences—likely not living to see my next birthday was one of them. I had accepted this fate, because my sacrifice would bring honor to my coven. Unfortunately, the prophecies were right. Obtaining The Power did result in my death—I became one of the creatures I had spent my life hunting.

I closed my eyes, focusing on my breathing. As a spirit user, I had a small affinity for all elements, but as a chosen one, a being who harnessed The Power, I had greater control. According to Sebastian, the only other vampire I'd met who shared my differences, that control was limitless, but he had yet to show me how to wield the gift.

I called upon the element air. A breeze swirled around me, fluttering through the thick locks that hung past my shoulders. I smiled as it sent shivers down my spine. As a vampire, I didn't feel cold in the same way I had as a mortal, but I still felt the sensation, and it was uncontrollably overwhelming. With my new, heightened senses, I could feel everything around me. It was as if the blindfold had finally been lifted, and after years of living in darkness, and even in silence, I could finally see, could finally hear. I had to die to truly feel alive.

As I brushed my palm against the dead grass I sat atop, I admired my handy work. I had been carving protection runes into headstones for hours and was due for a break. I knew the sun would rise soon, and with it, the remaining members of my vampire coven would slumber. But first, there was much to be done. Seventeen vampires from my new coven had fallen, including the guards of our coven's high priestess, Amicia. Jasik, my sire, explained that a burial had never been rushed. In fact, we were skipping key parts, but with Amicia missing, we weren't given the luxury of something as simple as time.

No one would talk about the likelihood that she had also been killed. Instead, my fellow Hunters and I put saving Amicia at the top of our to-do list and then called it a day. Ignoring the fact that Amicia was probably already dead didn't bother me as much as it should have. Being a Hunter, a vampire blessed with my very own set of superpowers, it was my job to protect my coven and the members within it. We had failed when she was taken. Saving her was the only way to redemption.

Though I focused on carving the thick lines into the headstone, my eyes kept flickering to the vampire beside me. Sebastian had offered his help—a ploy, I was sure. Nearly four days had passed since I threatened to kill him if he didn't tell me everything I wanted to know. He had brushed off my crassness with ease. Even now, as I watched him, he ignored me.

Lingering thoughts crept their way back into my mind. I remembered the dream I had the night I discovered we'd won the battle but lost so many in exchange. The Sebastian in my dream was nothing like the one sitting beside me. In my dream, he was cruel, evil. I was sure it was a vision warning me of what was to come. Being a spirit user, I had visions, but I had yet to learn control. I shuddered at the memory of the Hunters hanging from a tree, split open from navel to neck, their innards swaying from side to side as they hung, lifeless. Had I influenced it in some way? Was Sebastian lying in wait? I shook my head to clear my mind. I needed to remain focused on the task at hand. With one final stroke, the rune was complete. I stood, sheathing my knife and wiping the fine shards of rock from my hands.

"How much longer?" I asked.

"Done," Sebastian replied as he stood, his light, sandy-brown hair bouncing as he moved. It fell to just below his chin. His lanky frame towered over my short stature, though he wasn't quite as tall as Jasik.

I nodded, glancing around. We were attacked in this very place. Rogues, soulless, evil vampires who feasted on the blood of the living, had attacked my witch coven the eve of my birth rite and left me for dead. When they realized they'd failed to truly kill me, they came back to finish the job. Though I escaped again, others died in my stead. I closed my eyes, listening to the wind rustle the leaves. I focused on them but felt nothing. The world was empty. Our coven was broken. I hadn't been a vampire for long, but I was already drawn to them. It was powerful, unexplainable. They felt like family— family I had failed to protect.

I opened my eyes, ignoring the cheeky grin plastered on Sebastian's face. He had been with us for almost four days, and he had already gotten on my nerves. He was always watching me—just as I was watching him. He liked watching me tap into this power within myself, and even though he wouldn't admit it, I believed he liked knowing it was always just out of reach. I think he felt safer that way. No one but me had the power to truly hurt him. He knew that. Jasik knew that. I knew that. And it left a gnawing sensation in the pit of my gut. I didn't like being bested, and I especially didn't like being vulnerable.

I turned on my heel and walked the stone path that led to the manor's front door. My new vampire coven was hidden deep within rural Washington State. The forests of national parks surrounded us, keeping our existence secret from prying eyes. Each evening, I woke to crashing ocean waves and thick, salted air. It was nothing like home. My family moved from the remote woodlands of Wisconsin to the mountains of Shasta, California nearly a decade ago. I missed home. I missed Wisconsin and Shasta. I missed my family. But they had turned their backs on me when I needed them most— and now it was my turn to walk away from them.

I glanced back at the cemetery that was laid before our manor's front entrance. Thinking about how cliché my new vampire life was put a smile on my face when times only called for sorrow. Our gothic manor, painted with splashes of gray and black, sat on wooded property in the middle of remote land, and our front yard consisted of a burial ground and mausoleums. Now all I needed to do was turn into a bat, fall in love with a human, renounce my new destiny, and call it a day. I chuckled at the thought.

"What's on your mind, love?" Sebastian asked, his Australian accent coating his words.

I rolled my eyes. "Please stop calling me that."

Sebastian frustrated me to no end, and though I didn't fully trust him, I found myself questioning myself more. It was easy to fall into step beside him. I allowed myself moments of peace even though he was within reaching distance. This was a mistake I never would have made as a human, a witch. Why now? Was it my knowledge of the power bubbling within me? Was it his easy-going personality? Why did he affect me like this?

I opened the front double doors, and Sebastian closed them behind us as we entered. Vampires lingered in the conservatory and smiled softly as I passed. I smiled back as I took the grand stairs two at a time. I wasn't sure what our relationship was. They were my family now, and I had accepted that—even though, at first, there had been a lack of trust on both parts. My survival was dependent on them, and it seemed, their survival was dependent on me. We both needed each other in ways we didn't understand.

The double doors to Amicia's office were open. With Sebastian by my side, I entered, nodded to my fellow Hunters, and made my way to her desk, where Jasik sat, flipping through pages of a thick book. Dark circles were painted below his eyes, and he ran a hand through tangled hair. We slept in shifts after Amicia's abduction, but I suspected Jasik skipped his rounds altogether.

I cleared my throat, and Jasik tore his eyes away from the yellowed paper to meet mine.

"Is it finished?" he asked.

"Yes. The runes are carved, and the headstones are spelled. We can begin the ceremony at any time," I answered.

He released a quick burst of air—no doubt the breath he'd been holding since Amicia had been taken. He leaned back in the chair, running his hands over his eyes.

"I've been reading Amicia's journals for days and haven't found anything," he said, dropping his arms and straightening in the chair. "I only know my part and the basics. But it's not enough. It's been too long since we've..." It was an odd feeling: we were thankful for the lack of deaths, but the distance between the last burial ritual and now meant no one could remember the exact steps that needed to be taken. No one but Amicia, that is.

"We do what we can," Malik said. He looked just as exhausted as his brother. I knew it had to be difficult for Malik to watch his younger brother in such pain, even though the hard features of his face betrayed nothing. I was always amazed by Malik's ability to be completely and thoroughly unreadable.

"That won't be enough," Jasik said.

"Maybe we can do something different this time. I've done countless burial ceremonies. I mean, it's the least I can do," I said, hopeful.

"As much as I hate to say it, she's right," Lillie said, her Irish accent faint. She was sitting beside Malik, her pixie blonde locks in disarray. Her usual bright, blue eyes were red, puffy. We hadn't always seen eye-to-eye, but her confession didn't surprise me. We really didn't have another option. There were thousands upon thousands of hand-written journals in Amicia's library. After all, she was over seven hundred years old. A girl could accrue a lot of crap in that amount of time.

"I agree," Jeremiah said. I almost hadn't noticed him. Even now, he cowered in the corner, hiding in the shadows. "Besides, we need to get this over with." The harshness of his words struck anger in the others' eyes.

"Jeremiah—"

"I didn't mean—I just meant we need to hurry. The longer Amicia's out there, the more likely she's going to die. We just need to hurry and get her back, and then things can get back to normal."

"I don't think anything will ever be normal again," I said, meeting Jeremiah's sad, gray eyes. His dark chocolate skin turned ashy as he nervously scratched at his arms.

No one spoke. I knew we were all thinking the same thing: we couldn't go back to what we had. We had to move on, to let go. Opening our arms to the future and its possibilities was harder than we imagined.

"Okay. Avah will lead the burial, but it needs to be done tonight."

I nodded. "Everything I need should be in the basement stock room." I glanced at the clock. Still four hours before dawn. Plenty of time. "I just need an hour."

"We'll make the announcement while you prepare, then."

I left Amicia's office in a daze. Jasik rarely spoke of vampire law to me. In fact, my only experience with it had been when he had broken it to change me. I was on the brink of death, and I suppose he thought the sacrifice was worth it. The cost, he had explained, was death. Thankfully, Amicia granted him immunity. The day following Amicia's capture, Jasik had explained just how important it was to find Amicia: the Hunter's sole purpose was to protect his priestess. Failure would cost the Hunter his life. Bringing Amicia home, alive, was our only option.

I entered the basement quarters with Sebastian tailing me. It was easy to forget he was around—especially during the rare occasions he chose to remain silent. He was stealthy, invisible... almost.

"I don't need assistance," I said without meeting his gaze. I didn't like the power he held over us. He had information about what I was, and he had the strength that we could have used in battle. He had saved me, and I was grateful, but still, I couldn't stop thinking of 'what-ifs.' What if he had gotten there sooner? What if he had bypassed me and saved the others? What if...

"You sure? I've been to my fair share of burials, too." He quickened his pace so he was walking beside me.

I swung the door to our stock room open and walked inside. I discovered this room a few weeks ago, and it had become difficult to stay away. In it, we stored all things magical: relics, herbs, powders, oils, crystals, candles, books, and more. I remembered my first reaction to this room wasn't as pleasant. The elders of my witch coven had taught me that vampires and witches could—and would—never find a common ground. But since I became a vampire, that's all I've seemed to discover: a common ground.

"Want to help? Here," I said, grabbing some items from a shelf and tossing them into his arms. "Hold these." I grabbed the final pieces for our burial ritual and closed the door behind me.

Outside, I sat the items down beside the cemetery and began to work my magic—literally. The hour I spent cleansing ritual relics by passing them through the sage stick's smoke and setting up for circle seemed to come to an end almost as soon as it began. Behind me, black-clad members of my coven filed out of the manor and took the steps down toward me.

I smiled at my house-mates. "I know this isn't going to be the ceremony you're used to, but I promise I will do my best to honor our fallen. It is very important that you do not cross this line," I said, pointing to an invisible barrier. In truth, there was nothing there, but I couldn't allow anyone to break the circle. Had I had the time to learn control, I would have raised my own shield—one of my nifty vampire powers—as a barrier. "Sebastian will cleanse my aura and then join you."

I nodded to Sebastian, and he stepped forward, grabbing the burning bundle of sage. While I didn't fully trust his motives for finding me, I knew I didn't have another choice. Only a witch could speak these words, and besides me, he was the only one around.

"How do you enter?" he asked.

"With perfect love and perfect trust," I said. He waved the smoke stick up and down the length of my body. I turned so my back faced him, and he repeated the cleansing motion. I entered the circle, picked up my athame dagger, pressed the tip to the ground, and closed the circle. I walked to the center, where my altar sat. On it, I placed relics to represent each of our seventeen fallen members. Jasik and the other Hunters had chosen their memorial items. They brought pictures, cherished collectibles, and more.

I took a deep breath, calming the turmoil that raged within me, and then faced east. With my arm outstretched, I maintained my grasp on the athame and pointed the tip before me and toward the sky. "All that falls must rise again, and so, our friend shall be reborn.

The treasure of life is the air we breathe, that for which we will forever be grateful. I call to the gods of the east to bless this circle."

Still holding the athame, I turned and faced south. "As our life is but a day, our friend has passed into the night. Our strength, memories, courage, and the fires of our lives are given to us by our fallen friend. I call to the gods of the south to bless this circle."

The athame burned in my hand now as the power of my words fueled its energy. I turned again, this time facing west, and said, "As the sun sets, our friend has now left us. Our tears are like the waters of the ocean. I call to the gods of the west to bless this circle."

One final time, I turned and faced north. "As the earth has formed us, we now must return our friend back to that earth. We honor the gods for the life they have bestowed upon us and our friend. I call to the gods of the north to bless this circle."

My breath came in short, quick bursts, as the elements swirled around and within me. As they flowed into each crevice of my being, I smiled and silently thanked the gods. I may not have been a very good vampire, but I was a damn good witch.

I turned to face the altar and the remaining members of my coven, who watched with watery, wide eyes.

I raised the athame and pointed it toward the moon, saying, "You are the moon, Mother Earth, and the goddesses. Though you have fallen, you will remain an eternal creation, a life with no end, a never-ending cycle.

"You are the sun, the gods. You are born from us and will live through us. You only live and die to be reborn again. You are the destroyer, the ruler of the land of the dead.

"Bless our friends and see them safely into Summerland, where they will await their rebirth. May they be reborn again at the same time as the ones they have loved now, so they may know and love them again." With a final thrust, I twirled the athame in my hand and stabbed it into the cold, hard ground.

I stepped away from the athame, leaving it handle-deep in Mother Earth. I tore my teary eyes from the crowd and glanced at the seventeen candles standing tall on my altar.

"Incendia," I said, calling to fire. In unison, the seventeen candles sparked, their wicks igniting in flame.

"Though the wick on these candles will burn, the eternal fires within our hearts will never die. We say goodnight and goodbye to our fallen family, as they now must pass through Summerland with the knowledge that they will be missed and forever remembered in our thoughts and hearts. Blessed be, our friends, our family. May your crossing be peaceful and swift."

I grasped the handle of the athame and focused on its energies. The gods heard my plea and accepted our offering. The athame's handle, once burning with the power and energy I had left in it, now felt empty, a sign of acceptance. I pulled the athame from the ground, ending the ceremony. I set the athame on the altar and slowly raised my gaze. The others smiled at me with hopeful eyes.

One by one, the vampires walked to the graves to pay their respects. Most cried, and I found myself wondering just how long our fallen had been part of this coven's life. Had they been here since the beginning? Or were they newborns, their lives cut short by the burden of war? I was lost in my thoughts and hadn't heard Jasik approach from behind.

"That was beautiful," he said, pulling me toward him. I fell against his frame, resting my head against his chest. I closed my eyes and listened for his slow, steady heartbeat. The sound had been shocking when I first changed. I hadn't expected to find a heart, but I discovered that vampires had so much more than just beating hearts: like mortals, they had souls, desires, and downfalls. I opened my eyes to find Malik beside me, staring curiously.

"I was hesitant, but you came through. Thank you," he said before walking away, joining the other Hunters in the manor. Malik was very slowly opening up to me, and though I knew he needed time to accept the fact that his brother broke a vampire law of utmost importance by changing me, I still wanted him to just let it go. We had more important things to worry about, but had I said that to him, he'd probably simply tell me my ignorance betrayed my youth.

I stepped away from Jasik and wrapped my arms around my chest, watching as each vampire placed his or her hand atop a tombstone and spoke just above a whisper. They prayed that their loved ones would find their way home, and then they went inside, leaving their graves behind to seek shelter and comfort wherever they could find it.

"Sebastian refueled the protection spells around the manor," I said as I walked toward the front gate. "I just want to make a quick perimeter run to be sure everything's okay."

"I'll join you," Jasik said, grabbing onto my hand as we left the safety of the magical shield that kept Rogues from entering the manor while we slumbered.

Our manor was enclosed within a black wrought-iron fence boundary, and at each of the four corners, I had placed power-infused crystals to protect us. As we passed each now, I could feel its strength, power radiating from its points. Sebastian hadn't failed me. I wondered if I should consider giving him the benefit of the doubt.

"What's on your mind?" Jasik asked. I glanced up to find him staring at me intently.

"Nothing, really. Just thinking about everything—Amicia getting back, Sebastian and his many secrets."

"We need to discuss what we are to do," Jasik said, nodding.

"I think... I think he needs to join us when we begin tracking Amicia," I said.

Jasik came to an abrupt stop, turned, and faced me. I knew he wasn't going to like my suggestion.

"I think he'll be useful. We can keep an eye on him, and he and I can work one on one."

"Avah, it's not safe. We can't trust him. Not yet."

"If he wanted to kill me, don't you think he would have tried by now? Something? Anything?" It was true that I had lingering doubts regarding Sebastian's intentions, but admitting so would only fuel the fire Jasik was kindling. But I also couldn't deny that my faith in him held a stronger pull than my doubt. When it came to the unreadable Sebastian, I was left a mess of emotions.

"Not when he's facing a house full of vampires, an experienced team of Hunters, and you, but when we leave, it'll just be us. We'll be busy tracking, and you'll be alone with him."

"I don't need you to protect me, Jasik. I need to figure this out by myself."

Pain flashed in his eyes, and I immediately regretted my words.

"Jasik," I said, reaching for him, my fingertips lightly brushing against his skin, "I didn't mean it like that. I just need to figure this out, and I'd like answers sooner rather

291

than later. Besides, we can't just leave him at the house alone, unprotected. This isn't like your usual hunts. We'll be gone for weeks, not hours or days. They'll be too vulnerable."

"I've already contacted other covens. Each house is willing to send one Hunter here for protection. Our coven will be safe. The other Hunters will watch over him, ensuring he doesn't do anything he'll regret when we return."

"And you need to trust that I will be fine. I can do this. I can handle Sebastian. I can protect myself."

"Not against him. We still don't know his true power," Jasik said.

"But more importantly, we still don't know my power, and that's what matters. Besides, you won't need me to help you with tracking. I'll just be tagging along, really. So bringing Sebastian will give me something to do."

"Give you something to do? You speak as though saving Amicia isn't important to you."

I groaned and turned away but was caught by Jasik's hand. I yanked my arm free. "You know that's not what

I meant. Of course she's important to me, but she doesn't need me. I need me."

"I need you, too," he said, looking away.

In my frustration, I hadn't realized just how important this was to him. Sure, he wanted to protect me, but he was vulnerable, too. He had failed in his duties to protect his high priestess. His wounded pride needed tending. I just couldn't give him that. Not when I couldn't trust the growing, uncontrollable power inside me.

"I care a great deal about Amicia. You know this. Don't belittle my feelings just because I want to spend my days training with Sebastian while you four track her. I'll still be there. I'll still be with you. And I'll help whenever you need me. But I also need to think about myself. While I'm being there for everyone else, no one is being there for me, and I—"

He scoffed and turned away. "You can't be serious, Avah! Do you truly believe no one is here for you? Every vampire in that house," he said as he flung his arm toward the manor, "is here for you. They all trust you. They all want you to be part of this coven, and being part of this coven means doing your job as a Hunter. There will be plenty of time for training, but our first priority must be Amicia's return."

I was shocked into silence. Sure, I was being selfish, but after everything we'd been through, couldn't I be selfish for once in my life?

"Jasik, what's really going on? You know this coven has become one of my top priorities."

He ran a hand through his hair and exhaled deeply. "I just don't trust him. I just—I just want you to do this my way. I don't want to question your safety, and I don't want to worry about Sebastian. Not right now."

I understood completely. Though he didn't say the words, I knew where his hurt lay. Sebastian was the first vampire we'd encountered who shared my differences. Hell, he could be the only other one in existence. I was sure that bothered Jasik more than he let on.

I wrapped my arms around his neck. "You know my decision to bring him along is because I need to learn more about who I am and what I can do. Nothing more, and nothing less."

"And what happens once you've learned everything he can teach you?"

I shrugged, pulling him closer. "Sebastian will go back to Australia?"

Jasik closed his eyes and rested his forehead against mine. "When he's near... Everything feels different."

"What does that mean?" I whispered.

He shook his head. "I just... I don't know."

"Are you saying you feel differently for... for me?"

His eyes opened as he pulled away, and pain lingered there. "No. Of course not."

I nodded. His hand grasped mine, and he pulled me toward him. My mouth found his, and I leaned against him. Our bodies fit perfectly—each and every curve tucked neatly together. Hours could have passed before we finally pulled away breathlessly. I smiled up at him, his earlier unease gone.

"You're sure you can handle him?" he asked.

"Positive. I really think he doesn't want to hurt us."

"And if he does?"

I exhaled slowly, letting his words sink in. "If he does, well, then I'll take care of the situation."

While my instincts were telling me I could trust Sebastian, I couldn't deny the possibility that they'd betray me.

CHAPTER
TWO

AFTER MY ALMOST-tiff with Jasik, I went in search of Sebastian. The details describing just how we were supposed to find and save Amicia had already been decided, and plans were drawn out by the time Sebastian and I made our way into Amicia's office to meet with the other Hunters.

"Sebastian and I will be joining you," I said. I was eternally grateful to know that Jasik not only trusted me enough to let Sebastian join us, but he was also willing to set aside his leader tendencies and let me make my own decisions.

"We're what? I don't think so. I didn't come all this way to fight, sweet thing. Sebastian is staying here—

where there are comfy beds, food to eat, and bathrooms. I don't do the whole *nature thing*." Sebastian referring to himself in the third person put the strawberry icing on the damn cake he'd been baking all day.

"That doesn't surprise me," Jasik said.

I held back a chuckle and said, "They need me. Amicia needs me, and I need you. So you're coming." I hoped my tone conveyed just how serious I was. We didn't have time to argue.

"How do you expect me to train you while you're tracking?"

"I don't need to track. I just need to be there when it's time to fight. While they track," I said, pointing to Amicia's Hunters, "you and I will train. Maybe you can teach me enough to make a difference by the time we find her."

"This isn't a good idea," Sebastian said. His tone was serious, and I found myself wondering if leaving was the wrong decision. It was so easy for him to make me second-guess myself. I'd trusted and leaned on my instincts for years while hunting vampires.

They never failed me. But as soon as Sebastian opened his mouth, I was falling in step—in *his* step. I didn't like it.

"I second that. How do we know we can even trust him?" Lillie asked.

"But you're trusting enough to leave me here with the vampires you're meant to protect? You didn't think that one through did you, blondie?" Sebastian said. I rolled my eyes and met his gaze. I gave him my best *don't-tempt-her* glare before glancing past him. Amicia's office had large bay windows behind her desk. The manor was built on the far edge of a cliff that hung over the crashing Pacific Ocean. Slowly, the sky was lightening as the sun began to rise. If we were to leave tomorrow at dusk, then we needed plans set in stone quickly.

"Actually, I just thought we could lock you up until we get back and deal with you then," Lillie replied in her Miss America tone. She flashed him a wide smile.

"We're not doing that. Besides, I've been thinking about a locating spell, and to make it work, I'll need

Sebastian's help." I ignored Sebastian's frown.

"Do you really expect a tracking spell to work? They know you're part witch. Don't you think the Rogues thought you might do that?" Lillie asked.

I nodded. "But it's worth a try. So are you going to come willingly, or am I going to have to convince you?" I said, placing my hand on my sheathed weapon. I realized too soon that I was joking, and an uncomfortable feeling settled. Since when did Sebastian and I get on joking terms?

Sebastian barked out a hard laugh. "I love your enthusiasm, Avah. You act as though you really could take me. It's going to make you a fantastic asset."

I rolled my eyes and turned back toward the others. "So what're the plans?"

"There are four Hunters arriving just after sundown. Tonight, we rest and feast. Tomorrow, we hunt, and we don't stop until we've found her," Jasik said as he stood. He closed the journal and slid it back into its place on Amicia's bookshelf. The room was spotless. You couldn't even tell that we'd been ransacking the place in the hopes of finding answers.

"We should get ready, then," Lillie said.

"Yes, go to the armory and replace our weapons. Clean and sharpen the ones we cannot leave behind. When done, deliver them to our rooms, and then everyone needs to feed and sleep. We have a long day tomorrow," Jasik replied. Especially since we were racing the sun...

"Do we have any idea where we're going?" I asked.

"We're heading east. I assumed your old coven would have contacted you if they went south. We have friends toward the east, too. If we make it to them, we'll have a safe place to rest and feed."

I nodded. Jasik made it sound so simple. I was sure it was anything but.

Jasik closed the meeting, staying behind to speak with Malik, and we dispersed. Sebastian and I went to the kitchen, grabbed bags of blood, and feasted until our stretched stomachs ached.

"So when are we going to begin these promised lessons?" I asked.

"Lesson number one: consider a different diet."

"Huh?"

"Let me backtrack. First, I need you to promise you won't run and tell lover boy everything I tell you. Some things are better left a mystery."

"You know I can't promise that."

"At least consider it. Trust me."

I thought before responding. Obviously, he knew things I needed to know, and he wasn't going to give it up without a few conditions being met. "Fine."

"Good. Back to lesson number one," he said, leaning in closely as if someone were attempting to eavesdrop. "We can eat *real* food."

My stomach, now full from blood, grumbled at the thought of munching on candy, devouring a plate of pasta, and sipping on sweet tea.

"We're... like a hybrid species. We have all the perks of both with none of the weaknesses. Well, close to none. We're not invincible. Cut our heads off, and another isn't growin' back."

"So we can survive *without* feeding?" Though the thought of never needing to drink blood again made me want to shriek in excitement, I found myself wondering what that would really mean. Jasik had been questioning my vampirism since I turned. Maybe he had been right the whole time.

"Sure can. I only drink blood when I'm around covens like this. Those who don't know any better. I like to keep up the mystique."

"Why does that not surprise me?" I grinned, shaking my head.

He chuckled and swallowed down the last swig of blood in his blood bag, making dramatic refreshing noises. I couldn't help but laugh. The unease began to sink back in, and I decided then and there that I'd give him a chance. He was keeping his promises, and though he put up a fight when I'd told him he was joining us on the hunt, he was going to help find Amicia. I'd never been in the position to lend trust to someone I didn't know. At least, not until I turned. Becoming a vampire had me questioning everything I thought I knew and everything I thought I was. Why not continue with giving him a chance? If I was wrong, it'd only cost me my life...

"I like you, Sebastian. Please don't make me regret

that."

He winked at me. "I knew you couldn't resist my Aussie charm."

"I'm serious. This isn't a joke. Lives are at stake." I ignored his laugh at my unintentional pun. "And I'm going to need your help while we search for Amicia. I just need to know that I can count on you. You've shown me a different side of yourself since you initially arrived, and I want to make sure *that's* the Sebastian accompanying us on this venture."

"Relax, sweets. That's the only Sebastian I know. 'Sides, I do believe *you* were the one who was on the cranky side. Everyone seems to keep forgetting that *I* tried to *help* y'all."

"I know," I said, thinking back to the dream I had about Sebastian the night he arrived. I hoped it was anxiety and nothing more—especially since being around him was so easy, so natural. Briefly, I wondered what it would be like to have him join our coven. He'd definitely get along with Jeremiah if he were just given the chance.

When I met Sebastian's eyes again, his stare was

cold, harsh. He blinked, and it was gone. His annoying cheerfulness returned with a wink. I fought the urge to ask what had just happened, where his mind had just gone.

"I'm getting tired. Let's pack for our spells and then hit the sack," I said.

"Sounds like a plan, my little blueberry muffin." I was sure he had just resisted the urge to pinch my cheeks.

"I think I just swallowed vomit."

"The best part of being a vampire is the liquid diet. It tastes even better going down a second time," he said as he bent over in silent laughter, as if he was just way too funny to handle.

"You're disgusting," I said, but inside, I told myself I could get used to this. I could get used to Sebastian's bad jokes and awful pet names. I wasn't sure if I should be thrilled or horrified.

BACK IN MY room, I quickly showered and threw on

a clean pair of underwear. I smiled when I saw Jasik fast asleep on the bed. His dark hair was sleep-fussed, and his sculpted facial features left me licking my lips at the sight of him. Slowly, I crept over and slid in beside to him. He was nude, and his skin burned against mine. I didn't understand the allure he had over me, and honestly, I didn't care. I yanked the sheet back and admired him. His tanned skin was taut against his tall, muscular frame. I rolled on top of him, my legs astride, and rested my bare chest against his, as I softly kissed his neck. He moaned but remained sleeping. I no doubt had just gotten a starring role in whatever he was dreaming.

I sank my fangs into his neck, and his hands grasped my waist. His breath came in quick bursts as he grabbed onto the back of my head, tangling his fingers in my damp hair. He was grinding against me, hardening against my leg, and he held me tightly, pulling me closer as I drank from him. He tasted as sweet as candy, and I knew I could drink until he shriveled into nothing. I pulled myself away, a drip of blood sliding down the curve of my jaw and onto my chest. He leaned forward and began kissing the crimson trail down my chin. His tongue generously teased my skin as he made his way to my chest. Carefully, he began teasing my nipple until it hardened and lengthened in response. I moaned, grasping his head with my hands, exploring his hair with my fingers. I lightly pulled on his hair as I pushed him closer to me, and he furiously kissed my body in return. I felt him below me, hardening, lengthening. When I could no longer bear the sensation, I cried out to him. "Jasik, please." My fangs were throbbing now, begging me to explore him further.

In a swift motion, he was on top of me, trailing kisses down the length of my torso. When he reached my inner thigh, he looked up at me, meeting my gaze, his eyes burning a bright, neon blue, a showcase of his arousal. I bit my lower lip, dragging my teeth across the skin, knowing it would drive him mad. His hand wrapped around my frame, grasping my bottom fiercely. I inhaled sharply as he began kneading my skin, pushing me against his hardened limb. I grabbed onto his arms, running my fingers along his flexed muscles as he pushed me faster, harder against him. I felt the familiar sensation build within me, and I knew I was close. My body tensed, and he released me.

Angrily, I leaned against my elbows, staring down at him. A mischievous grin plastered across his face before he sank his fangs into my inner thigh, and I fought to control the pleasure erupting within me. I threw my head back and collapsed against the bed; my fangs lengthened again, their need making my entire body quiver. I felt his fingers lightly tease my skin just before he ripped my panties from me, the fabric falling to pieces as he tossed them to the floor.

Slowly, he inserted his index finger into me, and I writhed in response.

"Stay still, love. I want you to feel *everything* I'm going to do to you tonight." His words alone were enough to push me to the brink; I knew I couldn't hold on much longer.

He carefully inserted another finger and then pressed his palm against me, rubbing my sensitive nub as he pushed in and out, in and out. I cried out as

I clenched around his fingers, unable to contain the ecstasy any longer. He waited, plunging deeper, sucking harder, as I rode the orgasmic wave, until my heavy-lidded gaze met his eyes. He withdrew from me and slowly crawled up the bed, his arms on either side of me, stopping when his mouth reached mine. My tongue lightly licked the blood that trickled at the corner of his mouth. I tasted *good*. The thought shocked me. I pulled him into a deep, hard kiss. He met my kiss with equal ferocity. I dipped my tongue in to meet his, grazing past, exploring. He tasted better than anything I'd ever enjoyed. God, I wanted this man, and nothing could keep us apart. Nothing.

I pulled back, breathless. "Where have you been all my life?" The words escaped my lips before I'd even made the decision to speak them.

"Waiting for you…" he said fervently.

My breath caught. I had never loved anyone as much as I loved Jasik. Our love was new, inescapable. We'd fallen for each other almost as quickly as the gods had written it in our destinies. Our years of focus on the war left us inexperienced in love, but when he held me, I knew there was no place else I was meant to be. We fell fast, hard, because we were made to love each other.

I twisted so I was on top. I pressed a quick kiss to his lips and then angled my hips so that he easily slid into me. He closed his eyes, grasping my hips and moaning in response. Thick, long, and hard as stone, he filled me completely as I moved, slowly at first, up and down, taking pleasure in watching him squirm beneath me. Giving in, I quickened my pace until I had to grab the headboard to steady my movements. In unison, we lost ourselves in each other, our bodies shaking, sleek with dew.

I collapsed beside him and bit my lower lip. I could still feel the slickness of him within me, and the thought nearly drove me mad. I curved against him, gazing up at him with wanting eyes. I smiled wickedly and teased the skin around his navel with my fingertip.

"You, Milady, are insatiable," he said, staring at my taunting mouth.

I turned so that my head rested against his

shoulder and inhaled deeply, taking in his scent. He smelled of sweat and blood and his own unique musk. It was intoxicating, and I knew I could take him again. Now. And he wouldn't stop me. We'd lose ourselves in each other if we could—if we could see past the responsibilities plaguing us.

"I think I'm going to take a walk," I said, sitting up, suddenly needing air—and to get my libido in check.

He nodded. "Be careful. Sun." He spoke sleepily and just above a whisper.

I smiled at him as I cleaned myself and dressed. By the time I opened the bedroom door to leave, he was in a deep sleep.

"CAN'T SLEEP, SUGAR lips?" Sebastian said as I walked into the downstairs parlor.

"Seriously? Sugar lips?" I said, shaking my head as I took a seat beside him. "What are you doing in here?" It was nearly dawn, so the vampires of the house had long been asleep.

"I like it here. It's quiet during this time of day. No one to stare or ask questions. It's *almost* as close to peaceful as we can get."

"Almost?"

A sly grin formed. "Ready for lesson number fifteen?"

"Fifteen? I think we skipped a couple—"

"Nonsense," he said, waving a hand. "I'm a fantastic mentor. You're getting the best damn education money can buy."

"I'm not paying you, Sebastian," I said.

"Tsk. Tsk." He wiggled his finger at me. "Details. We'll cover those later. So?"

"Let's move on to lesson *fifteen*." I rolled my eyes and held back my chuckle.

His sly grin molded into a full-on cheeky smile as he stood, grabbed my arm, and yanked me out the front door. He stood behind me, covering my eyes with his hands.

"Sebastian, what are you doing? It's almost sunrise!"

His lips brushed the back of my ear, sending shivers down my body, and he whispered, "Not almost." My heartbeat increased, echoing almost painfully in my mind as I considered his words.

As he lowered his hands, his fingertips lightly brushed against the curve of my jawline. I opened my eyes quickly, without hesitation, but was blinded. I brought my hands up instinctively, and as my eyes adjusted to the light, I removed their cover. I kept my hands before me, staring at my palms. The heat from the sun that blared down upon us was so warm, so comforting. I felt like I was back home in Wisconsin, sitting beside a fireplace as my father told me stories of the demons that walked in the night. I thought I'd never see the sun again.

"How is this—"

"Possible?" Sebastian said. "All things are possible now, Avah."

"It feels—"

"Amazing? Like nothing you've ever felt before?"

I nodded, my breath quickening. My heart was beating rapidly. I closed my eyes and listened. The creatures that embraced the night were long gone, sleeping in their beds, no doubt. The world was filled with new sounds from creatures I had forgotten. Birds chirped, squirrels ran through the forest, and deer pranced through the brush. The beauty of the world had been just out of reach for so long.

"The beauty of the world is never out of reach, Avah," Sebastian said, and my eyes shot open.

"How..."

"Look deep within you. You already know." He stepped closer, eliminating what little space was between us. I was acutely aware of his proximity. My hair seemed to stand on end.

"We have them all, don't we? All the Hunters powers?" I said.

"We do," was all he said.

When Sebastian arrived, his first instinct was to save my life, while mine was to put up walls, become defensive. I was overly cautious, as I had been trained to be around vampires. After settling for a day, and after allowing myself to feel more at ease around him, I had asked him what brought him here. His answer was simple.

"You brought me here, Avah," he had said.

"How?" I had asked, but he simply smiled and walked away, leaving me a confused mess. I didn't chase him and demand for an answer, because I was too afraid of what it might be, now, his words hung over me.

"Sebastian?" I asked.

"Hmm?" His eyes burned with hunger.

I swallowed the lump in my throat and asked, "What brought you here?"

His mouth curved into a small smile. "You."

I shook my head. "What does that mean?"

"One day, I woke, and all I could see was you. Your face haunted my days, my nights, my dreams... Whenever I'd glance into my future, I'd see you smiling back at me. I knew I had to find you. I had to find the girl who took my breath away every time she looked at me, every time she smiled my way, every time laughed. I was meant to find you, to be here with you."

My breath caught at his admission. I couldn't deny

that there was something lingering between us. I didn't understand it, but I knew he was right: he was meant to find me, to be here with me.

He placed a finger below my chin, raising my head so that I met his gaze, and then he leaned down and brushed his lips against mine. I pulled away.

"What are you doing?" I said, stepping back. "I'm involved. You know that."

"Can't blame me for trying, right?" he asked with a boyish grin.

Frustrated, I moved farther away. I rested against the railing, crossing my arms over my chest as I stared at the sun. So much had happened: I learned the sun wasn't a threat, I confirmed I had all Hunter abilities, and I discovered that I was somehow part of Sebastian's future.

"I can't believe you did that," I whispered. In actuality, it didn't surprise me that he made a move. But did he have to choose the worst possible moment to do it? I closed my eyes, allowing myself to bask in the sun. Its warmth covered me in waves. "You took this moment from me—a moment I've wanted since I turned. How could you? Now every time I remember the day I re-experienced the sun—"

"You'll think of me."

I groaned and opened my eyes, pushing past him. "I'm going to bed, and don't even think of making a surprise visit. I'll stake you before you can even make a move," I yelled over my shoulder.

I retreated to the sounds of his low chuckle.

ABOUT THE AUTHOR

Danielle Rose is a romance writer and owner of Narrative Ink Editing LLC. She holds a Master of Fine Arts in creative writing from the University of Southern Maine and a Bachelor of Arts in English from the University of Wisconsin—Parkside. Danielle currently resides in the Midwest, where she spends her days dreaming of warmer temperatures.

When not writing, reading, or traveling, Danielle can be found teaching composition at her local university or penning her next novel at a local coffee shop.

Visit Danielle online: www.Danielle-Rose.com.

Also by

DANIELLE ROSE

Daemon Academy

Coming soon...
BLOOD BOOKS TRILOGY
Blood Magic
Blood Promise

SECRETS & SHOTS TRILOGY

Vexes & Vodka

Tricks & Tequila

Wishes & Whiskey

PIECES OF ME DUET

Break on Me

Before I Fall